In My Hand
a Forest:

book one of
The Seed Series

by D.H. Richards

DEDICATION

For our children – Avery, Isaac, Henderson, Jacob

Hurley, Ava, Kayla, and Harris.

You are our greatest treasures.

CONTENTS

{preface}

when mother earth is hungry

she lays bare her mountains and valleys

ready for the taking

the wind does its job

carrying miraculous pods of life

scattering their promises like tender kisses

over all of her awakened surface

mindful of any neglected terrain

clouds come to cover her

molecules of vapor rubbing together faster

and faster

as they hover over her beautiful frame

eager to impart their energy

and satisfy the longing

to bridge the gap

between sand

and sky

she smiles and opens herself to the heavens

welcoming their advances

with patches of fertile ground

that beckon and tease

harnessed electricity is released

in a cataclysmic burst of lightning

shocking the atmosphere

penetrating the earth

finding home deep within her

again and again

seeds burrow into the lining

joyfully receiving each quivering drop of rain

joining in the holy conception of

life

mother earth laughing with pleasure

mist settles into her arms for the night

and she sighs

satiated

trying not to appear too content

in the silvery afterglow

of barren moonlight

CHAPTER 1

Ellie's toes felt numb in her leather boots as she plodded through the sodden leaves on the bank of the river. The long and wet winter had made this Tuesday seem like any other, an infinity mirror of time in either direction, a remembering and anticipation of nothing but cold, gray rain.

Her woolen hood created a little amphitheater of sound for her ears, curving around her head with serendipitous acoustical precision; and though she did not want to be walking home – *home? Could it be called "home?"* – she at least took respite in the concert being performed for her by the forest as she ambled along. She could hear the gentle *plop! plop!* of fat raindrops collecting in pools on leaves and in hollows, the water going through the motions, part of the endless cycle. The dripping from the trees above reverberated like little tapping gunshots as they landed on her. The squish of her shoes on the muddy trail ran up against the sounds of the river in soggy protestation. Scoggins Creek couldn't truly be called a river, but Ellie detested the way her mother pronounced the word "creek" – *crick* – and refused to call it anything but.

The weekly walk home was a one-hour journey, give or take, and Ellie's calves and arches had grown strong because of it, though she hardly cared about that. One hour, alone, every week, slogging along in the cold, and all for what? To enable her mother in her crazy ways, only to then have to turn around and walk the hour back the next day. Ellie's fingers wrapped around the phone in her pocket, her thumb worrying the upper edge of her screen protector and anticipating the moment she could plug it in, recharge the very dead and nearly useless battery, and feel connected to the world like a normal human being. Her backpack was weighed down with water and her jeans were quite soaked around the ankles. The thought of a warm blanket by the fire while checking her feed and texting her friends sounded about as close to heaven as she dared wish for.

A chickadee skittered unexpectedly across the path directly in front of her, causing her to suck in her breath. The smell of moss, pine, and ferns filled her lungs and partially soothed away the scare. She stopped for a moment to watch the bird arrange its wings after hopping up onto a blackberry vine, deftly grasping between the awful thorns. Its black and white striped head shifted about before it called out – *chick-a-dee-dee-dee* – and flew away. *You are lucky, little bird. Take me with you.*

It was close to noon, which in the Oregon winter means that

the sun, if visible at all, is in the sky to the south at the exact angle needed to cause blindness to any poor soul foolish enough to glance in that direction. The rain had taken a small break but was threatening to soon resume. Ellie shielded her eyes against the intermittent blast of filtered sunlight, finding herself grateful for the thin, gray clouds despite the weather they tended to bring along with them. Her stomach growled. She was getting closer to home.

At the fork in the creek she made her way across the water on top of the fallen tree that created a convenient natural bridge. The spongy moss covering the trunk helped keep her feet from slipping out from under her as she shimmied sideways, finding her balance. She hopped down on the other side and hiked up her jeans.

It was usually at this point that her feet reminded her of the blisters that hadn't quite healed from the weeks prior and were sure to continue torturing her sixteen-year-old frame. She hoisted herself up the rocks at the top of the ridge, finding awkward footholds that never seemed to get any easier from week to week. If she was careful to exit the trees where she and her father had measured and marked, she wouldn't be seen by the neighbors as she approached the barn.

Sometimes she wanted to just come rolling out of the trees, down the hill like a child, screaming and laughing all of the way down – *Who cares? So what, they see me – who cares?* – but the someone who truly cared – her father – was no longer there to fully explain why. He was no longer there to fully explain a lot of things, and for that reason Ellie's defiant teenage heart was kept in check, at least for this one request.

She gazed down at the rear of their family land while still safely hidden away by the pines, rubbing her fingertips on the bark of the trunk nearest to her. *Father.* The wide fields to the south of the barn were mostly barren now after two years of neglect. No one could blame them, of course, with no father and only Ellie, Mara, and their mother to tend to farm chores. Ellie's eyes swept over the small garden of raised flower beds which she still tended to, bringing at least some signs of life to the place. This time of year, not much was growing by the way of flowers, but she had a fine assortment of bulbs beginning to poke their green heads from the earth. Ellie looked at the slowly graying white boards of their two-story farmhouse and a pang of nostalgia washed over her. More than anything she just wanted to be home and for everything to go back to the way it was before.

Gaston, Oregon is a town full of proud, self-proclaimed pioneer stock who live and die by the timber industry. None too religious, the people are not ashamed of the town's raucous past or casual approach with the Almighty. The community church built in 1873 passed through multiple clergy's hands and the white clapboard exterior bears the stains of mud, moss, and many years of the residents' sins. *Church isn't for perfect people,* they would say. *Ain't for imperfect people, neither.* Ellie always wanted to go inside the church every time she passed by it. She was curious as to what she might find. Things in the world had changed, though, and it had been many years since a congregation had graced its doorways.

The road running in front of their home was not visible from the ridge, but Ellie still listened for any sounds of cars or people before scurrying down to the side of the barn and skirting around its edge just as she had for what felt like countless Tuesdays. As she approached the back porch, she reminded herself to act normal in case the neighbors happened to be watching from a window. She could be seen now. The point, now, *was* to be seen.

Ellie mounted the two steps to the covered porch and lifted the little stone frog to retrieve the key. She unlocked the door with a familiar *clunk-shunk* and propped it open while she set down her backpack on the bench in the hallway. The drizzly rain was starting up again and a rumble of far-off thunder greeted her as she disturbed the spiders seeking refuge in the firewood outside the back door. She carried in an armload of the logs she quartered last fall and set them in the bucket next to the fireplace in the sitting room off the kitchen. She closed the door and breathed in the familiar smell of old varnished wood and carpets that needed vacuuming. It usually took until evening for her nose to get readjusted to the new-but-familiar environment.

The old antique mirror in the hallway piqued her vanity, and she spent some time examining herself in it. Her icy blue-green eyes stood out against her dark lashes. Her kinky, dark auburn hair was exuberant in the humid air, much to her dismay. A map of freckles marked a path across the pale bridge of her nose. Ellie paused to worry over a pimple she could feel forming on her chin. Her rosebud lips were slightly blue in the cold, which reminded her that warmth was near and only waiting for her.

Grabbing the matches and a handful of newspapers from the paper bin, she set about creating a fire in the fireplace, her favorite of all chores. There is such satisfaction in building something and watching it burn – watching the paper take light, the flames burning it away with a rush of heat and passion, hoping the baptism of fire is enough to burrow some embers into the heart of the wood for a long and slow burn, glowing red, eventually becoming black and white char. *All things are simply matter, Ellie. Matter cannot be destroyed. It simply shifts into a different state. See those ashes –*

There was a sudden jolt in Ellie's stomach. She fell back from her haunches and sat on the wooden floor with a thud. She was not sure what had caused herself to startle. Had she heard a noise? No. Had something touched her? She was alone. It was a feeling inside that one gets when they have a sudden remembering of something they have forgotten, causing her insides to drop as though she had leapt from her bedroom window. *The window!*

The prior Tuesday had been a rare sunny day and she had relished the opportunity to open her bedroom window to circulate some fresh air. She meant to close it before trekking back to the berm house, but Ellie now remembered that she hadn't. Ellie raced up the stairs to her room and threw open the door, afraid to see the mess that was likely to be found after a full week of the elements having their way. When she sprung into the space, however, she was surprised to find everything dry and tucked away neatly, the window closed.

Ellie stood still, taking in the scene. Had she simply forgotten closing it? Had she folded her blanket that way? She tried to remember. She couldn't. She felt relieved but nervous. *I must have forgotten*, she told herself.

Ellie's nose reminded her of the task she had walked away from. She followed the scent of burning paper and wood back down the stairs, chastising herself for leaving a fire unattended. Her efforts had been successful. A hot tongue of flames licked at the carefully stacked kindling inside the woodburning stove. She checked to make sure the flue was open to draw out the smoke. Once the fire had burned long enough and hot enough, Ellie slowly closed the cast iron door, anchoring the handle and locking it down. She peered at the orange glow through the soot-covered window.

This was always her favorite part of the weekly walk – the end. The part where she got to kick off her shoes, grab something to eat from the pantry, pull the soft armchair over in front of the woodstove, plug in her phone, and feel connected again to a somewhat normal world.

The cuisine of choice this week was canned peaches. After pulling a bottle down from the pantry shelf, she paused to see her mother's handwriting scrawled on the top before opening the jar in the kitchen and spilling the sweet, wonderful contents into a ceramic bowl. Ellie snatched a fork out of the top drawer next to the sink, got herself situated on the overstuffed chair, and dug in with her left hand, scrolling on her phone with the right.

Are you home? she texted Hazel. Her phone battery had only a trace of life left and was struggling to connect to the weak cell signal at the farmhouse. *Weak signal is better than no signal,* she reminded herself. Ellie laid her phone down to charge, figuring she would eat and let it have a chance to have enough power before trying to see what her friends had been up to online.

As she ate her peaches she thought about when she and Mara had helped mother to can them. It had been a banner year for peaches – *a real humdinger/Dad I hate that word* – and father had proudly come home with four full boxes from the farm around the corner. "Four boxes!" mother had exclaimed. "Good Lord."

They smiled and kissed each other. That time, Ellie didn't hide her eyes.

They had all been in the kitchen together, each with sleeves rolled up and fingers armed with a paring knife. The five-gallon bucket father brought in from the barn was quickly filling with fuzzy peach skins as they sat with their chairs circled around it, bent forward, elbows on their thighs, peeling away. Mother showed them all how to halve the peach with a single slice. She then would twist the halves apart and dig out the pit with her strong fingers, toss it into the bucket, and set one peach half in the bowl by her feet. The other peach half she would hold in her left palm and carefully use the paring knife in her right hand to scrape the tip of the fuzzy skin from the very top. Separating it bit by bit from the juicy flesh until about half an inch had been gently pulled away, she would then grasp the flap of peach fuzz against the knife blade with her thumb and forefinger. With a steady, confident motion she would pull the skin all the way down and off of the fruit, leaving behind a perfect, unmarred dome of peachy goodness. Most of the time she could get it all off in one go. By the end, Ellie's peaches usually looked as poked and prodded as they truly had been – but mother's peaches were always flawless, peeled and sliced to perfection, the bright red centers bleeding out their love for her. Father would hold her waist with his strong hands while she lifted the hot, boiled jars out of the canning pot, setting them on a towel on the counter to cool before screwing the lids down tighter and placing them in rows in the pantry. He would kiss her neck and she would stop still and close her eyes while he did so. She would breathe and he would breathe, and the world was soft, and the shelves were stacked with gold.

i

inside a small gossamer bag, closed

by its own self-cinching top

lay a seed

on a shelf

inside of a larger paper bag

in the dark

dessicated and shriveled

it waits to be reborn

reincarnated

again

and again

as it has every season

for untold number of years

what do you know

hibernating child

what have you done

before you were even born

before you were even

conceived

an egg inside of your mother

inside of her mother

matryoshka doll genetics

from generations far gone

still live

in you

what wars have you seen

what tombstones have your tendrils

wrapped around

whose pocket have you traveled in

and from how far

away

little seed

what mouths have you fed

down the ancestral line

lead by a legacy so real

and so fine

that your anatomy

can scarcely

be traced by a mere season alone

the world lives in you

and in me

you are me

and they

and we

in one

a single seed from

a single seed

and still there are millions of you

being born

living

dying

but not a true death

'tis but a sleeping

a quiet and patient waiting

to be pressed into the earth

thirsty

CHAPTER 2

Ellie woke with a start. The fire had died down and was sending a menacing glow out into the darkened room. She sat up straight from her slumped position in the armchair. The gales of wind that had picked up outside seemed to blow right through the seams of the house and into her bones. She reached out for her phone to check and see what time it was, her fingers scrambling around until she could grasp the familiar hard rectangle in her hand. She held it up to her face – still dead. *What?* She checked the charging cable, pulled it out and put it back in. Nothing. *Is it connected to the wall?* She followed the cord in the darkness over to the outlet and found it fully plugged in.

Ellie stood and felt along the wall for the light switch as her eyes adjusted to the dimly lit space. *Windowsill...curtain...light switch!* She flicked it up, hoping to finally be able to see and reorient herself in the world.

The light did not come. The darkness stayed, and her confusion mixed with drowsiness did her a disservice, causing her mind to run in circles. *Am I dreaming? Am I home?* Her eyes were beginning to adjust to the almost extinguished firelight. She got a couple more logs from the gusty back porch, a few more handfuls of paper, and set about building the fire back up. The paper was slow to light, and the smoke was filling the space. She checked the flue and found it closed. *How...I know I opened it...didn't I?* She pushed the flue rod back in, allowing the rush of air to suck the smoke up and out the chimney. The influx of oxygen caused the embers to glow hot and then burn out immediately.

Ellie stood up from the woodstove and headed for the emergency cabinet in the hallway. The dim moonlight was just enough to help her make out the cupboard handle. Her hands searched around until they felt the familiar shape of a flashlight. She grabbed it and flipped it on, the steady beam of light flooding the space with distorted and long shadows. Feeling better that she could now see around herself, Ellie went from room to room trying the light switches. None of them worked.

Ugh. Mara...Probably got so busy that she forgot to pay the electric bill. Ellie pictured their mother back at the berm house, probably staring off into space, mumbling her weird chants while sitting in the rocking chair with her long, graying hair cascading over her shoulders in frazzled little knots. *Just brush your hair, Mother. It isn't hard.*

Ellie did her best to wash the dish that had held her peaches in the kitchen with the flashlight balanced on the counter, the beam of light focused up in an effort to illuminate the room. As she dried it with a kitchen towel, she tried not to think of the prospect of being alone in a house all night with no power. *I mean – your eyes are closed anyway, right? No big deal.*

Ellie placed the bowl back in the red cabinet and grabbed the flashlight before heading to her room. She knew it was only early evening, though the winter sun was already down. She knew she hadn't eaten much, but the unsettled feeling in her veins wouldn't allow for much else to be ingested. She was still tired, teenage tired.

She mounted the creaky steps of the back staircase leading up from the nook off the kitchen, reaching the landing that allowed you to either continue forward and down the front staircase to the sitting room with the fireplace and puffy chair or upstairs to the bedrooms on the second floor. Her flashlight danced along the family portraits on the wall as she continued upstairs, the eyes of the past following her from their framed prisons.

As she slept, they watched her through the walls, waiting.

{-------}

The walk into town the next morning was uneventful, save the flittering thoughts skipping around Ellie's mind. She had started out an hour earlier than usual, hoping to stop by the library before going to the ARC. She clung to her phone in her pocket, the charging cord still plugged in and wrapped around it in the way Mara hated. *You'll ruin the charging port doing that/I don't care.* She could think of little else when thinking of her dead phone battery. It caused great anxiety to feel so disconnected from the world here at the farmhouse. At the berm house she was used to it. As she walked, fretting about her phone, she greeted the people she passed on the street with sixteen-year-old dismissiveness, most of them too old or too young to be bothered with.

Rounding the corner of the library, she popped into the entrance, took a right down the hallway, found herself a bean bag chair close to an outlet, plopped down and took great pleasure in the buzzing green lightning bolt that appeared as she plugged in her phone. Setting her backpack down beside her and taking a big breath of relief, she reached over to the side table for a teen magazine and lazily thumbed through it. She paused on an ad for hair styling products and consciously played with her frizzy curls, overly aware of how long it had been since they had seen the likes of gel or mousse or hairspray of any kind. *Not like I have anywhere fancy to go.* She turned the page and started reading an article about preparing for college. The teens in the accompanying photos were all fashionable and thin, and the girls wore glasses to make them look smarter. Home high school was already torturous enough, so why anyone would add the drudgery of home university was beyond her. Ellie hoped to finish her graduation requirements as soon as possible and then never be bothered with school again.

It wasn't that she disliked learning – far from it. She adored gathering new information and applying it. What she couldn't stomach was the structure of school itself. Mind you, she had to be her own taskmaster in all things school related as Mara was living away at the ARC. Mother was, well – *useless,* and Father was gone.

That is the word they would always use, *gone.* Not dead, not missing, but gone. She supposed that it felt the safest of the three. Easiest. If someone is dead, you are compelled to grieve and move on. If someone is missing, you are compelled to keep searching. If they are simply gone you are compelled to do nothing at all.

Out of the corner of Ellie's eye she saw a boy enter the room and the energy surrounding her shifted. She was on high alert without wanting to be, overly aware of his tall and muscular presence, trying to steal glances in his direction while appearing as though his being there didn't affect her in the slightest.

A quick look here, a feigned scanning of the room there, and she was well on her way to making out her first impression of this new individual.

Or was he new? There seemed something entirely familiar

about his dark hair and blue eyes. Ellie tried to think of where she may have seen him before. Where would it have been? Ellie didn't go very many places and hardly interacted with anyone at all, so it was incredibly bothersome to her that she could not place her finger on it.

After a reverie that went on for more minutes than Ellie was aware, she snapped out of her fog and looked around. The familiar boy with a jawline of steel was gone.

Ellie made note of the strange disappointment that she felt, a feeling she had not felt before. This was not a feeling like when Christmas was over or when she finished reading the last page in her favorite book – this was something different. She was not entirely sure she liked it.

Ellie checked the status of her phone and saw the time – 9:37 with her battery at 47%. She gathered her things into her backpack and made her way outside under the rumbling clouds, annoyed with herself for eyeing the sparse crowd of library patrons for signs of the boy.

Nothing. He was truly gone.

{-------}

The ARC had been established two years prior, when Mara was sixteen and Ellie just fourteen. Mara had been intrigued by it from the beginning, poring over the literature she had picked up from the library.

"Mom, look," she had said, pointing into a brochure that said *Agricultural Research Corporation: Together we Succeed.* "They provide everything I need there. I work for them – for *us* – and in return I have a place to stay, access to schooling, clean clothes – and the whole family gets extra food as a bonus."

Mother continued to stare out the window, humming. The purple floral house dress she had been wearing for a week was unraveling at the hem, but still looked beautiful somehow on her slender, soft silhouette. The sheer fabric seemed to breathe with her – *in, out, in, out.*

"I'm almost done with my high school credits. I can just finish them up there at night." She pointed into the pamphlet. "They even have one-on-one tutoring there. Maybe I can finally get a grasp on writing a passable essay." She smirked. "And I can kick their behinds in calculus if needs be."

Mother's vacant expression didn't change, but her eyes shifted a little, the usual sign to show she was getting restless. Soon she would be going around the property to gather the cats and talk to the moon, scooping their hissing bodies up into her arms. "*Thig dhachaigh thugam,*" she would chant in her grandmother's Scots

Gaelic, a language neither Mara nor Ellie knew or wanted to know.

Mara bent low to look Mother in the eyes. "I'm going to go, Mom. I will do this." Their mother had a rare moment of connection, meeting Mara's gaze, and nodding. "I know," she whispered. A faint smile turned up the corners of her mouth as she reached out to tuck Mara's hair behind her ear, a motherly gesture so missed and so welcome that it caused Mara to breathe deeply and close her eyes against rapidly forming tears. Mother turned to Ellie, her unbrushed teeth bared in a desperate plea. "Eliyah will never leave me."

Every time Ellie made the weekly trek from the berm house to the farmhouse she would hear her mother's voice echoing in her mind as she walked. *Eliyah will never leave me.* Why did she have to say that? Why did she have to make her feel so trapped, so laden with expectation? Why was it fair that Mara got to go away, leave behind the craziness and antiquated lifestyle, and Ellie was expected to stay the same, never to be free of this life that had been thrust upon her?

Ellie arrived at the ARC and pulled open the glass main entry door. The heavy metal handle was cool in her hand, which caused a shiver to go up her spine on this gray and drizzly day. She entered the sterile, sealed concrete lobby, the cold floors squeaking in protest against her wet sneakers. The lobby was vast and tall, able to hold long lines of people snaking back and forth as if awaiting a ride at an amusement park, though Gaston had a scant seven hundred people. Cheerful music played over the speakers at a comfortable volume. Everything was neat and in order, always. Workers like Mara were constantly sweeping and cleaning, changing out trash bins, changing the batteries in the clocks on the walls, checking the baskets and carts for any discarded or lost items. The order inside was a contrast to the general decay of the town outside.

Even though she arrived at the entrance just before ten a.m. Ellie knew she would be one of many already waiting inside. The ARC used to make everyone wait out in the weather, but after the first very cold winter they changed their policy and started opening the doors at nine-thirty to allow the people some respite from the chill. It only helped a little, as the lobby held very little capability to hold warmth of any real significance.

Ellie always felt a little guilty being able to bypass the long main line. That was one of the perks of having a family member working there – a dedicated, shorter line. Today she came up to the window and smiled civilly at the new young woman posted there.

"Your name?" she asked Ellie.

"Ellie Coleman."

"And your family member's name?"

"Mara Coleman. My sister."

The girl seemed to flinch at the mention of Mara. Ellie

22

studied her unfamiliar face for signs as to why her sister might be cause for discomfort. Mara was the kindest, most gentle human Ellie had ever known. She could never imagine her causing purposeful harm or pain to anyone.

"Are you new here?" Ellie tried to make small talk as the girl typed into the keyboard, searching for Ellie and Mara in the database.

"Depends on what you call 'new'," she replied. She turned to grab a card, scanned the barcode and waited for the screen to flash a green 'Approved' before picking up the phone on the wall. "Family pick up for Mara Coleman. Family pick up for Mara Coleman." Ellie could hear her voice being spoken over a loudspeaker in the back warehouse. The girl then buzzed Ellie through a door to the left and gestured for her to wait on a bench against the wall for Mara to come and meet her. "She'll be here momentarily."

"Thank you," Ellie said as she slid her backpack off of her shoulders and sank down onto the frigid metal. She tried to remind herself that in the hot summer this icy bench was a luxury, so to save her shivers for another time. She looked at the image in front of her, one that had become so familiar on these weekly walks. The long rows of tall, stainless steel shelves heading straight back for what seemed like forever, holding box after box of things like bagged beans, bagged rice, and canned vegetables. The shoppers, led around by an ARC employee, placed the allotted amount of bags for their family size into their carts, neat and orderly. The rows were expertly organized so that as one shopped you would come upon the heaviest, bulkiest items first and end on the most fragile of items like eggs. The employees consulted their clipboards. The shoppers spoke very little.

Banners were hung on the walls with the ARC's ideals proudly stated. On one, *Everything You Need.* On another, *Feeding You Feeds Us.* Ellie's favorite, *Working Together to Feed the World,* was the largest of the banners hung across the end of the four middle aisles high above their heads. The signs were well designed with a pleasing color palette of muted earth tones and interesting graphics and gave the feeling of being in a tourist destination.

It made Ellie remember riding in the car to the coast, stopping at the Tillamook cheese factory for curds and ice cream when she was five or so, Mara eight. The signs made it feel so important, so special. They had taken a picture by the big main sign. Ellie had smiled through a chocolate ice cream goatee. The beach had been warm. Mother was laughing. Mara got sunburned. Father had stood back, observing, watching them play in the sand like he was recording everything in his mind, to be played back later. He often did that.

"Ready?"

Mara's voice brought Ellie back to reality. She looked up,

happy to see her sister's familiar face surrounded by her dark honey blond hair that was pulled back into a bun. They had both started life with that honey blonde color, but Ellie's seemed to seek for independence, only growing darker every year. "Yes! Hi. I am."

Mara gestured toward the first row with her head and shook her clipboard expectantly. "It's goodie time!" she chirped.

Ellie knit her brows together. "Goodie time?"

Mara laughed. "Whatever. Food time. Be boring."

Ellie stood and picked up her backpack, setting it into the cart that Mara grabbed from the front corral by the far wall. They headed toward the first aisle. Ellie was glad to have someone to talk to, even if only for a little bit.

"What is with that new girl up front?"

Mara shrugged, pointing to the top, ten-pound bag of flour for Ellie to place in the cart.

"It's just, she got, like, weird or something when I said your name." Ellie obediently placed a bag of rice in the cart when Mara pointed. "It was…weird, I guess. Just thought you should know."

Mara shrugged again. "Some people just aren't cut out for ARC, I guess. Some kids only stick around for a few weeks. I don't know why – it is pretty sweet here."

They traveled the rest of the first aisle in silence, Mara pointing at items and Ellie placing them in the cart as Mara checked them off on her clipboard. As they turned the corner to the second aisle Mara pointed again.

"Three cans of green beans."

Ellie felt her phone buzz in her pocket and pulled it out to check for a text from Hazel. She was disappointed to find it was simply an update notification.

"Do you want the green beans or not?"

Ellie opened her eyes super wide and stared straight at Mara while slowly reaching over for the cans and very slowly placed them in the cart as if moving through molasses. She hoped to annoy her sister enough to get her to smile first.

She not only smiled, she laughed a big hearty laugh and pretended to smack Ellie across the face. "Knock it off."

"What?" Ellie said. "I'm always excited about cans of green, edible seed packets."

For the rest of the shopping trip Ellie talked to herself, mostly, but she could tell that Mara was happy to listen.

"Oh, get this. I was at the library this morning."

Mara shot her a puzzled look.

"To charge my phone. Which – what is going on at the house? The power isn't working. I had, like, no light last night and that sucked. Did you forget to pay the bill or something?"

Mara pointed to the peanut butter. "I don't know. Maybe? I'm sorry."

"And that wasn't fun after walking and getting soaked for an hour."

A familiar voice came through the space between boxes from the next aisle over. "Those Coleman sisters, always causing trouble. Where were you walking from?" Ellie and Mara shifted to see Jack Rowland, a longtime family friend and the town sheriff, peering through the gaps and smirking beside his shopping cart. Ellie laughed. Mara shook her head playfully, but Ellie could see her fingers worrying the edge of her clipboard.

"You know us," said Mara. "A couple of regular rebels." Ellie's ears bathed in the sound of her sister's voice. She didn't realize each week how starved she was for Mara until she was in her presence. She missed her sister terribly. She put her arms around Mara's waist and hugged her, taking Mara by surprise.

Jack – or as the girls had grown up calling him, Sheriff Jack – seemed happy to see them. "How are things going over at the Coleman house, Ells-Bells?"

Ellie's eyes shifted. "Going well, I guess." Why did they have to pretend like they still lived there? All of this was so dumb.

"And your mom?"

"She's good."

"Doing a little better?"

Ellie shrugged. "It seems so."

"That's good to hear." Jack adjusted his collar. "I came by early yesterday to check in, seeing as I hadn't heard from either of you for a while. I knocked, but no one answered."

Ellie could feel Mara stiffening by her side. "That's usually when Ellie takes Mom out for a walk, right Ellie?"

Ellie did her best to play along. "Yes, usually. Or sometimes we just sit out on the back porch. Get some sun. So, yeah."

"It was raining all yesterday. Pretty hard."

Ellie nodded, not sure what to say.

"I just worry if she's not doing well, being out in the cold and rain…that can't be good for her."

"We had an umbrella." Ellie wanted this conversation to be over.

Sheriff Rowland nodded and tipped his head, then pointed the direction he was being led by his shopping helper. "If you need anything, just holler. Tell your mom I said hello."

"I will," Ellie called after him.

The sisters watched him walk away through the gaps. Once he was out of earshot, Mara said, "Dang, girl. Watch yo' mouth." She put her arm around Ellie's shoulder as Ellie rolled her eyes at her sister's choice of words. "No talking about your hour-long walks, okay?" She gently rocked the both of them side to side. "Let's get to the next aisle. The new hot chocolate mix is pretty *dope.*"

Ellie smiled at her big sister. "You're such a nerd."

ii

It is hope

that is the beginning

of all things

a thought

of what is

to come

a seed is planted not

with the vision

of seeds in mind

but

the *fruit*

you see the garden

full

and lush

ready to harvest

you taste the melon on your tongue

feel the fuzzy lima bean pods

hold the warm, sun-cracked tomato in your hand

long before you press

the seed

into the earth's waiting womb

CHAPTER 3

The trip back to the farmhouse from the ARC was always arduous. Ellie's backpack was one of the kinds that have wheels and a handle for pulling, so that helped, but the other bags had to be slung over her shoulders and they dug in something fierce. The farmhouse was only a couple of miles away. When dragging groceries, however, it felt like a million.

Ellie made a right-hand turn onto Sequoia Drive as the backpack sounded its repetitive *shunk, shunk, shunk* over the seams in the sidewalk. The rain was shy now, sending tiny droplets here and there, but nothing major. The work of carrying everything made Ellie feel hot and out of breath anyway, so some rain wouldn't necessarily invoke complaints. The nice homes in this newer development stood tall amid the landscaping that still needed a few years to fill in. Ellie's stomach growled in anticipation of lunch as she plodded along.

The sound of fingers tapping on glass caught her attention. She looked up to her friend Hazel peering out from her living room window and waving. She disappeared and then reappeared in the doorway, coming down the front walk to greet her, her short brown hair bobbing above her dark eyes, which most definitely did not match her name.

"Holy angel buns! Look at you. You're like a bag lady or something."

Ellie snickered. "Yeah. Literally."

"I cannot wait until I'm sixteen and can drive. I have my permit, but, you know, I can't drive my friends and stuff. Do you have your permit? Here, put those down inside and come hang out for a bit. I never get to see you. Later we can beg David to drive you back home so you don't have to carry all of that." This plan sounded very agreeable to Ellie. She would only stay for a little while.

As they carried in the groceries Ellie was hit with waves of nostalgia and envy. She took in the smell of the Dixon home, something so familiar to her, even in their new house. It smelled like a mixture of fresh bread, clean laundry, and comfort. She looked at the finely appointed foyer table and was enveloped by the beautiful, orderly home they kept in all its decorated glory. The environment was a far cry from the Coleman farmhouse, let alone the berm house. Being so suddenly immersed in such splendid, warm perfection caused her to be very aware of her own slovenly appearance, and she stopped at the hallway mirror to smooth her unruly hair. She lined her shoes up next to Hazel's by the door that led to the garage and prayed no one would notice the holes in her mismatched socks.

Hazel placed the bags of food next to the pantry door and put away the refrigerated items as she talked. Ellie took a seat at one of the kitchen barstools, thankful for the rest. The television played quietly in the adjacent family room. A commercial for the ARC came on, and Hazel's parents appeared on the screen. They had very white teeth. Hazel rolled her eyes and made a sound of disgust.

"I am so sick of seeing this. I hate seeing my parents on tv. It's gross. They're gross. They are at some ARC training thing until late tonight. And - I totally walked in on them making out the other day."

Ellie smiled and reached for the bowl of cashews on the counter. "Whatever. Old people don't make out."

"Except that they *do.* And it's disgusting. The worst part? My parents don't even think they are old. I mean, I guess compared to some they look better, but I don't know. They're old. It's gross." Hazel placed the eggs on a shelf. Their fridge was very clean. The glass shelves sparkled. "Anyway, what have you been up to? You've been pretty quiet on the chat."

Ellie shifted on the barstool. "I don't know. Doing school stuff, I guess." She picked at her jeans. "I saw someone today. At the library."

Hazel made a face while getting the bread down to make some sandwiches. "Ooooooh, a *someone?*" She made her eyelashes flutter. "Or, like, a *someone?*" She made a crazy face. She laughed. "I don't even know what that means."

"No, like – well, it was a boy." Ellie's ears started turning red.

Hazel set the bread down on the counter. "Continue."

"And that's it."

"What?"

"I saw him, and it was like two seconds, and he wasn't there anymore."

"Like a ghost?"

"What? No. I mean, I don't even know…it was weird."

"Huh." Hazel started slathering the bread with peanut butter and jelly. "If seeing a random boy at the library for two seconds is the highlight of your week, we have problems."

Ellie cleared her throat. "Yeah. I mean, I'm focused on school and stuff. Want to get done early." Ellie gratefully took a bite of the pb & j that Hazel handed to her on a plate. Hazel took a bite of her own.

They ate in silence for a bit.

Behind them, the news talked from the television. *The government has announced a new program for those with unused land. Have a lot you don't use or can't take care of? Or perhaps you inherited acreage? Well, you can now give that land to the government in exchange for tax forgiveness. Chief Correspondent Amy Withers has more.*

Hazel made another of her signature disgusted noises. "Boring." She used the remote to turn the tv off and opened the freezer. "Do you want some ice cream or something?"

Ellie was still chilled from being outside. "No, thanks." She ran to grab something from her shopping bag and held it out. "I wouldn't say no to a hot chocolate, though."

{-----}

David's car rumbled down the bumpy road that led in front of the Colemans farmhouse. Ellie was in the backseat with Hazel, looking out through the dusky rain, a pit in her stomach for having stayed too long at their house.

Mother would be expecting her back that night, like usual, but the sun was almost down and Ellie knew better than to try and find her way in the dark. Ellie knew "expecting" meant something different when it came to her mother.

She actually wasn't sure if her mother ever even noticed when she was gone.

She would simply need to stay another night and return in the morning. As soon as she made the decision, however, she somehow knew her mother *did* notice and was busy panicking – a spider string between a mother and a daughter, stretched so thin and so long that it made the silk vibrate with awareness.

Hazel had been chattering on and on the entire ride, which was only a few minutes long. When they reached Ellie's property, David slowly turned down the gravel drive that led to the side of the house.

"Hello, old house," Hazel said, waving out her window at the house next door where the Dixons used to live.

Ellie was embarrassed by the weeds in the farmhouse driveway that were shining in the headlights of David's car. She hadn't realized how far she had let the property go, how bad it looked to others until this moment.

Her father had always tried hard to keep things as nice as one could in a place like Oregon, where nature is constantly encroaching on civilization.

Tourists "oooh'd" and "ahhh'd" over the abundant wild blackberries and the ever-present greenery and moss. Locals scrubbed and sprayed to get the ghastly green off of their walks and roofs and fought in vain to uproot the satanic blackberry vines from their gardens.

Ellie grabbed the handle and hopped out of the car, intending to carry her stuff in quickly and send them on their way before they asked too many questions. David was already loading a bag onto his shoulder, though, and insisted on carrying it inside. "Which door?" he said, smiling his goofy smile. His curly blond hair twisted down his forehead in a playful poof.

Ellie pointed to the back door that led straight into the kitchen. She and Hazel got the backpack and other bag out of the trunk and followed David toward the back steps.

"Be careful – sorry, I don't have the light on. I didn't expect to be out this late." Ellie slipped on a rock and caught herself.

David lumbered up the couple of steps to the back screen door and pulled it open.

"Oh, wait – that door is locked, I need to – " Ellie began.

David opened the door easily and shuffled in, laughing.

"Look who forgot to lock up?" he whispered, aware that it was dark inside the house. Ellie thought back through her day. *I was sure I locked it.*

They all crowded into the small and dim dining area, setting their bags on the table. Hazel reached back to turn on the light. Ellie's stomach dropped when she remembered – *no lights.*

"Oh – is the lightbulb out in here?" Hazel asked.

"Yeah, I guess. I'll change it. Don't worry about it. Thanks for coming."

Hazel didn't listen to Ellie's hints to leave enough alone and went to the hallway and flipped that switch.

"Huh. Your lights aren't working."

"Huh. Weird. I'll figure it out."

"We aren't leaving you here in the dark, Ellie," said David.

He ran back out the door and returned a minute later with a flashlight he had grabbed from his car.

"Always prepared," he said, patting himself on the back.

His big teeth couldn't stay caged by his lips most of the time and this moment was no exception. In the harsh beam of the flashlight his face looked distorted and strange, no longer belonging to the kind, curly-headed pseudo-brother she had always known.

He opened his eyes wide and placed the flashlight under his chin. "I *vant* to suck your blood!" he said, the most pitiful vampire you have ever seen. His curls were highlighted by the bright light, looking wild and electrified. Ellie laughed and Hazel rolled her eyes.

"Oh my furballs, David! How do we fix it? Besides – don't we need to be quiet? For your mom?"

Once, when she was thirteen, Ellie had taken a pot and a wooden spoon and stood outside her mother's open bedroom door. Mother had been staring out of the same window all day, rocking back and forth on the end of the chair beside her bed. Ellie had tried hard to get her to look at her, to look at anything else. She banged the pot with the spoon – *Clang! Clang! Clang!* and her mother began to cry. Mara scolded her. Ellie hid.

"Oh – yeah – she's probably in bed already. She tends to go up pretty early." Ellie wondered if Hazel could see through her lies. Maybe the darkness made them more convincing.

David traveled through the first floor, testing the switches, finding them all not working. "There's gotta be something going on with your power, Ells. Where is the fuse box?"

"The what?"

"Yeah, David. We don't know stupid grown up stuff," said

Hazel.

"It's a box in the wall that you open up that has switches inside for your power," David explained patiently. "Haven't you ever tripped a fuse and needed to reset it?"

"Ew! Stop! We're just kids, okay?"

"Well, I will remind you of that when you want me to take you to get your driver's permit."

"That's different."

David shrugged his shoulders. "If you can't reset a breaker, you can't handle driving a vehicle. It's just reality."

Ellie put her finger to her lips, pointing upstairs and making use of her family's lie to get them to stop bickering.

"Oh, yeah – sorry, Ells." David gave a furtive glance up the back staircase.

"Okay, fine, David. What does a flipping fuse box look like?" Hazel crossed her arms over her chest, strange shadows dancing across her face.

The girls helped him to look and they finally located it on the wall just outside the pantry. It was hidden behind some aprons and dish towels hung on hooks. Ellie pulled them to the side and David showed them how to slide the latch and open the panel.

"Super easy," he said.

When he shone the flashlight on the breakers, he was taken back. "Oh," he said. "Huh. That's weird."

"What?" said Hazel and Ellie in unison.

"Normally if you trip a fuse, the breaker is hanging out halfway between off and on. You have to switch it to off and then all the way back to on to reset it. These breakers…they're all off. Like, *off* off."

Ellie tried to figure out what this meant. "Like, the whole house?"

"Yeah…all except one." He consulted the diagram that was scribbled to the right. Her father's handwriting. Ellie's heart hurt. "It's the fuse that controls the fridge. That's lucky."

"Ellie, are you just messing with us?"

"What? No!"

"All the power is turned off except for the fridge. You wanted to scare me but didn't want your eggs to go bad. I get it." She playfully pushed Ellie to the side. "You fuzz nugget."

"No! I didn't…"

"Ha *ha,* Ellie. If you didn't, who did? Your *mom?*" David's goofy smile was back.

"Yeah, why would she do that?" piped Hazel. "It had to be you, so just give it up already."

Not being able to grasp what this really meant for her and feeling it easier to just play along, Ellie pulled a silly face and pointed to herself. "You got me."

Hazel shook her head as David got all of the breakers reset. "I would blame this all on cute library boy going to your head if I didn't know that you saw him *after* leaving home this morning. Still. This took some planning."

"I don't know. I guess I got bored, or something."

"Cute library boy, huh?" said David, switching on the light in the dining area around the corner. The artificial light flooded the space and felt so foreign to their eyes that had long adjusted to the dark. Ellie's ears were growing red again.

"Thanks for helping carry the food in, guys. I'm calling it a night."

Hazel and David waved as they let themselves out.

"Have fun with library boy in your dreams," teased David. "Don't check out too many books together."

iii

how welcome is water

to a parched soul

one who has been

dessicated

dried

and dulled

the wetness finds its way

into the hard folds and cracks of the seed

seeking out its flaws

to flood them

drowning in equal parts misery

and joy

the imbibition of moisture

overwhelms and tears the membranes

with the sudden influx

of potential.

CHAPTER 4

It was almost ten in the morning as Ellie entered the small valley where their berm home was situated. The weather had decided to be remarkably hospitable for a late-winter-early-spring day and she was grateful for the respite from rain. It still had been a slog to get home, but at least she could keep her head high and had no need of her hood. In fact, halfway through her journey, as she kept in the trees behind the old mill, she had paused to take her jacket off altogether and stuff it in her backpack. Hurrying faster than usual had brought up her heart rate, and her pulse warmed her through.

She had had a fitful night, tossing and waking every twenty minutes or so. She felt like she could hear her mother crying, worried, screaming at times. Her mother floated through her dreams and tugged at her hair and whispered in her ears until she could no longer stay in bed. She got up and tested the lights, just in case. They worked.

She tried not to think about the lights as she walked. She tried not to think about a lot of things.

That mysterious boy had woven himself through her dreams, too. Every time he came into her dreams, she felt a dark warmth come over her. Every time he left, that same, strange yearning she felt at the library would follow. Like a part of *her* was leaving. She was frustrated that she was dreaming about someone she had literally only caught a glance of. She didn't even really have a face solidly in her mind to place on him, just a foggy composite of characteristics. Strong jaw. Icy blue eyes, like her own. Dark hair. Tall. In her dreams she didn't so much *see* him as *feel* him. She just knew it was him. A presence that felt familiar yet excitingly new at the same time.

Now she placed her feet down one after the other, over and over, worrying what scene was to greet her upon entering the berm house. She could see the house coming nearer as she walked. It was a beautiful scene, albeit humble in terms of modern housing. The hills on either side sloped down into a wide valley of low growing grass. The Oregon winter had greened the world beautifully, and the emerald ground stood in contrast to the mostly leafless deciduous trees. The evergreen pines stood tall and majestic and filled the atmosphere with the most incredible forest air. Off to the right was the berm house, nestled into the embankment. The house itself was nothing to look at, being a true berm house cut into the side of a small hill. They had placed three shipping containers side by side for the base structure. From there, father had finished it the best he could to modern standards. She still remembered the ten-year-old fear she had felt as he cut holes for doors and windows in the steel, the saw sending out sparks in great starbursts of light. Mara had done her best to comfort Ellie, but the reality was that she was afraid, too. There were solar panels on the south-facing ground past a small grove of trees that helped to hide their ugliness. Since they had no television, internet, or electronics of any kind the power they generated went mostly to lights and appliances. Mother had refused to go without a well-appointed kitchen and laundry room. *And you know how happy I can make you when you make me happy* she had said, dancing with him in the living room at the farmhouse, their noses touching, his hand in the small of her back.

Ellie could now see the steam from the laundry room vent spilling into the cold air. *She's doing laundry. That's new.* Ellie's heart hoped that this meant her mother was feeling well, that things were going to be okay, and that the fact that she had spent an extra night away from home would go quite unnoticed. She approached the imitation wood-grain steel front door and took a big breath. The familiar round doorknob felt large in her hand. *Hobbit house.*

Ellie's first step inside the door greeted her with the usual scene – spare but functional furniture, everything appearing to have been acquired from disparate thrift stores, but cozy nonetheless. The living room was situated around a red oriental rug that had had its tassels cut off by Mara. *They always get sucked into the vacuum cleaner and they're ugly, Mom!* This room, in general, stayed exactly the same year-round. The ugly, tufted pea-green chair with a barrel back stood closest to the window, with the brown leather wingback chair coming next, just to the left of the fireplace. The rose-colored sofa that always smelled faintly of curry graced the opposite side of the rug. They all faced inward to a rectangular, honey oak coffee table from the 1980s. It was bulky and rounded and beveled with gold. In the center of the coffee table lay a massive copy of *The Seed Garden: the Art and Practice of Seed Saving.* That book and countless seed catalogs had always been part of the family, even at the farmhouse. Some children remember Dr. Seuss or Eric Carle as the books of their childhood. Ellie remembered pictures of fruit and vegetable plants with their romantic names – *Gill's Golden Pippin, Rooster Spur, Moon and Stars.*

A sound from the kitchen startled Ellie. Pots and pans were clanging together and a most wonderful smell of garlic and potatoes was filling the space. Ellie was surprised to find her mother at the counter, peeling and chopping potatoes and onions. She was showered and dressed in clean clothes that were covered by an apron. She was humming and skirting around the island to wash her hands at the sink under the garden window. The kitchen had been scrubbed into submission and the surfaces gleamed, still emanating the smell of lemon cleaner. Unsure if her mother had seen her enter the room, and unsure of how to feel about this abnormally normal scene before her eyes, Ellie quietly lowered her backpack to the floor and waited to be addressed.

Her mother stood with her back to her, still washing her hands at the sink as she began to speak. Her long, brown hair was combed and pinned back at the sides.

"I see you made it home."

"Yeah." Ellie's fingers fidgeted with one another. "What are you making? It smells really, really good. Can I help?"

Her mother's head fell back in a silent bout of laughter. She dried her hands with a dishtowel and turned around, placing her hands on the island and leaning forward. Her head dropped down, and then shot back up, her eyes drilling holes in Ellie.

"Do you know how worried I have been?"

Ellie shifted uncomfortably. "Yeah."

Her mother waited for more of an explanation. "That's it? Yeah?"

Ellie averted her eyes and shrugged. "It was what I had to do. It got late. Things took longer than usual yesterday, and I didn't want to walk home in the dark. So I waited until the morning."

"Things took longer? I would say so."

"Why are you being so angry at me? Shouldn't you just be

glad that I am okay?"

"Are you okay?"

Ellie was taken back by this passive-aggressive question. "Yes. I am obviously okay." She waved her arms and legs around.

"Who did you see on your trip?"

"What? No one. Just, whatever – the regular people I see. Like always." Ellie's anger began to brew. "You know, I do *everything* for us. I live here alone with you, I walk to the farmhouse alone, I stay there alone, and I go to the ARC alone. I'm a prisoner, just like you want me to be."

Her mother shook her head. "You are so spoiled. You take all of this for granted. You have no idea..." she trailed off, placing her hands on either side of her face. "Nobody asked you any questions? Seemed...suspicious?"

"No. No one asked any questions. No one is suspicious. They think I am weird, yeah – thanks to you and all of your crazy rules! I don't know why we have to do any of this!"

"And Mara – she seemed...normal?"

"Well," Ellie paused. "She was a little more quiet, I guess. Than usual."

Her mother became heightened in her stance, ears perked.

"Quiet?"

"She just seemed, I don't know, tired or something. And she didn't want me to talk to Sheriff Jack when he asked about you."

"Jack asked about me?" Her mother fidgeted. "You said no one asked any questions!"

"Well – what do you expect, Mom? He just said to tell you hello. No one has seen you for a really long time. People are going to be…curious."

"So they *are* suspicious." She pushed away from the counter. The water on the stove was boiling. She looked at the rolling bubbles and started to go away again. Ellie could see it, feel her going away.

"What? Mom! They just worry, okay? Here I am saying the same lies over and over again – *She isn't feeling well. She goes to bed early.* – whatever! It's weird. This is all weird. No one else I know lives in a hidey-house in the mountains while pretending to still live in town. We're weird, and it's stupid, and I'm over it!"

Her mother kept staring at the boiling water without any expression.

"Mom."

Nothing.

"*Mom.*"

Her mother began to mumble something under her breath. *"Thig dhachaigh thugam,"* she said, over and over. Ellie knew the window of normalcy had closed.

She turned off the stove and led her mother by the hand to the back sitting room, untying and removing her apron before helping her into her favorite chair by the window. Before Ellie knew what she was doing, she reached out and grabbed hold of a lock of her mother's hair and yanked it. Her mother's head jerked down with the forcible tug, but no recognition spread across her vacant face. Her head slowly turned toward the sunlight, eyes combing the land outside the window as she almost inaudibly said, "Go away."

Ellie felt the force of those words ripping into her heart. She backed away from the window and turned to run out of the room, out of the house, out of the situation that caused her to feel so closed in, so detached, so used and unappreciated.

Her feet carried her swiftly back across the valley of grass and toward the river. Her hot tears spilled down her cheeks even though she ordered them not to. She didn't even bother to wipe them away as she ran, her pulse thundering in her ears, her feet *shunk shunk shunk*-ing into the ground.

She didn't stop until she had rounded the bend at the head of the river, slid down the embankment, and treaded across the mossy rocks at the narrow neck just above the first small falls. She sat in the hollow of an old cedar tree and hugged her knees to her, her forehead resting on them as she cried. Her tears were beginning to slow now, but the sadness was steadily growing. It was an angry sadness. This chance she had had to speak with her mother, to interact with her in a regular, normal way, had all been ruined. By what? Who knew when and why she chose to disappear, go away in her mind, leave the care of everything else to Ellie. *I shouldn't have yelled at her/This is all so stupid/She deserves to be yelled at/You are not a good daughter/I should have let her burn the house down.* The voices in her head fought and sought for blame, for understanding, for justification of her anger and for evidence of her guilt. *I shouldn't have yelled. This is my fault.*

Ellie raised her eyes and let them gaze, unfocused, at the forest trees ahead of her. The rush of water was usually such a soothing sound, but in this moment of emotional unsteadiness, it roared in her ears like an accusatory white noise. She didn't have to try very hard to dull her senses as the aftermath of crying included an empty exhaustion, similar to that she had experienced after her father died. *Did he die? I don't know. No. Maybe.*

She let her breath take over, a steady in, out, in, out with a few shudders between. She knew she would return. She would go back to the berm house and find a way to feed her mother something, walk her through the motions, help her get ready for bed. She knew she would feel bad about it and angry about it and tired of doing it and also proud of caring for her mother. She had to be the adult. It was the only way. It was life now. And she loved her mother. She loved what was left of her.

She had been staring out at the trees for what felt a very long time when she heard a twig snap to her left down the riverbank. Expecting to see a rabbit or maybe even a deer, Ellie turned her head and was startled to see a boy – *that boy* – meandering her way.

Why was he all the way out here? Had he seen her? Does he know? Should she hide?

There was no way she could hide at that point. He was about twenty feet away, much too close to attempt an escape.

She stood up from the cedar hollow and brushed off her dirty jeans, very aware of her rough appearance and hoping her tear-stained face had had enough time to return to a semi-normal state. His eyes, which had been focused down at his feet, lifted at the sudden movement in front of him.

They stood looking at each other as if they each had been caught doing something they shouldn't have been, unsure who had been there first and who was in whose territory.

His dark hair was disheveled, and his golden skin was smudged on one cheek. He was wearing jeans and a dark gray hoodie with laced up boots that had seen better days. He had on fingertip gloves and was holding a tackle box in his left hand and a fishing rod in his right. He reached up with the back of his right hand to wipe across his cheek, the fishing rod sweeping out in front of him like a safety bubble. His gloves left behind a bigger smudge. Ellie smiled, sure he had no idea.

He smiled and nodded.

Ellie nodded back.

A painful silence separated them for a few seconds, until they both started talking at once.

"I'm not used to seeing –"

"You're quite a ways out here –"

Another pause.

"What?"

"Oh – sorry, I…I didn't expect to run into anybody. You kind of spooked me."

Upon hearing his voice Ellie could feel her whole body come alive.

Spooked me? Who says that?

She tucked her hair behind her ears, and then, remembering that Hazel said that made her ears look bigger, promptly pulled her hair back out again.

"Yeah, well I could say the same."

He looked amused. His blue eyes twinkled. "Do you want me to leave?"

He has dimples.

"No," she said, a little too quickly. "I mean, you can if you want to, but, no – it's okay."

He looked around, not seeing a bag or fishing rod or anything of any outdoor use. "Do you need help or anything?"

Realizing it did look a little strange for her to be out there on her own, she decided to play it cool. "Just…relaxing. I like…hiking. And stuff." *Oh my goodness, Ellie, shut up shut up shut up.*

He put out his lower lip, thinking. "I think I'll be heading up over there," he said, pointing up the river. "There's a spot I found yesterday that the fish like to hang out at."

"Okay. Cool." *No, don't leave. Don't make me want to follow you.*

"What did you say your name was?"

"Ellie. Well, Eliyah, but everyone just calls me Ellie."

A look of surprise came into his eyes. "No way." He set down his things and came close to her, a kind of close that was uncomfortable and delicious at the same time. "Eliyah?"

Ellie's heart raced as he looked her straight in the eyes, searching. Ellie was confused but would gladly stay confused for the rest of her life if it meant being close to this mysterious, beautiful boy. He was a good six inches taller than her, maybe more. She awkwardly shifted her weight, not wanting to look away but afraid of looking too deeply into him. She had never looked at a boy this way.

"*Ellie*," he said. He gently grabbed her left hand, and lifted the fingertips to press against his own, like a tent. His thumb moved back and forth as it touched hers. Her heart stilled as her mind made the connection, going back in her memory to pull this person from its depths and bridge the gap of so many years.

She saw in her mind a garden, *her* garden at the farmhouse. Ellie was eight years old, and it was the first time she had been given her own plot of land to tend. *Learning to grow a plant is akin to godliness*, her mother would say. *The Earth is our keeper, and we must be Hers*. She remembered digging happily in the dirt, turning in the rich black compost the day before she was to plant her first crop of peas.

The garden was surrounded by a decorative wooden fence she had painted white with her father. He had cut the wood pieces from an old dead tree on the property. They nailed it together and painted it all in one day. They then put in a gate and stapled chicken wire to the back of the fence to keep out the rabbits and other critters that would surely gobble everything up. One side of the fence was adjacent to the neighboring property. It was always quiet over there, and the neighbors grew a thick cover of holly and laurel along the entire fence, making spying on them an impossible game. She had tried many times during afternoons of boredom to catch a glimpse through the leaves, but the laurel was unyielding, and the holly poked her in a horrible way when she tried to reach through the chain link and part the hedge.

One particular spring day as she sat digging in the compost, she heard a sound from behind her. She turned to see a small boy, about her age she guessed, probably a little older. He had dark hair and piercing blue eyes. He said nothing as he crouched behind the neighboring fence, no doubt uncomfortable between it and the mean plants. His ratty blue jacket seemed thin, and he folded his arms across his chest to keep from moving too much.

"Does that hurt you?" she said. He didn't respond. She took a look back to the house. The laundry was swaying on the line but mother was nowhere to be seen. She stood and walked over to the fence. She crouched low to be able to whisper to him. "I'm eight years old."

"I'm nine and three-quarters."

"What is your name?"

His eyes flitted away, then came back. "Charlie."

"My name is Eliyah. It's like Elijah, you know, in the Bible."

She asked him to put his hand through the fence. He refused, shaking his head.

"Okay, just go like this then." Eliyah put her fingers up to the fence, each one finding its own place in one of the hexagonal openings of the chain link.

He smiled a small smile and blinked. Slowly, his hand came up to meet hers. Their fingertips pressed against one another. They smiled at each other, then began to push back and forth on one another's fingers, children discovering a new game, a new friend.

With a big thrust, Charlie sent Eliyah backwards onto her behind. She laughed as she fell. A voice was heard calling out.

"*Charlie! CHARLIE!*"

Charlie's face froze as he realized he would be caught. He sat, resigned to his fate, as a woman with gardening gloves and frizzy black hair pulled ferociously at the ivy and lifted it to reveal his hiding place.

She stared at Eliyah with disgust, and then at Charlie with an equal distaste. "Get away from there Charlie. Never speak to them again!" She pulled his arm hard, dragging him out from the ivy.

Eliyah could hear him crying as she walked away with him, scolding in a hissing whisper as they went.

The movement of his hand brought her back to the present. She let her hand drop to her side as she studied the features of his face. The dark hair, the blue eyes, so blue! His strong jaw and cheekbones were obvious indicators of his older teenage status but there still remained a boyish softness about him, something about his demeanor, his mouth. She didn't feel afraid to stare.

"Charlie?!" she squealed. She felt her body moving toward him as if for a hug, and all the alarms within her started screaming, *No! No! He'll think you're weird! Stop!* She instead playfully pushed his shoulder and her entire being registered the muscled, strong frame that could be felt under his knit clothing.

They hadn't seen much of each other after that first day in the garden, but they had found other ways to communicate and remain friends. Though the overgrown fence separated their entire back yard and part of the front, there was a tree halfway between their properties near the street. A sucker had been pruned from the spot where the trunk split and as the tree grew it had formed a small, round hollow like a hand cupped and waiting for treasures.

Soon after the fence incident, Ellie had written Charlie a note that said *I found this rock. Do you like it?* She folded it up and placed it under the rock in the tree, and then played close by until she had seen his face pop up in an upstairs window. She pointed at the tree and then ran when she saw his mother's stern outline nearing a downstairs window.

Later that afternoon she had watched with delight from her living room window as he neared the tree and first took a furtive glance back at his home, then at hers. She waved. He inspected the tree and quickly found her gift, clutching it and running back inside.

They had passed notes and treasures back and forth undetected like this for a year or so until Charlie's family had moved away.

Ellie had not known they were moving.

From what she could tell reading his notes in the weeks prior, he had had no idea, either.

One morning in the bright spring Ellie had gifted him a robin eggshell and a few sugar snap pea pods from her garden just before she and her family had gone to work on the berm house for a couple days. When they came back, Charlie's family was gone.

The next family to move in had been the Dixons. Ellie made fast friends with Hazel, and all was right with the world. She never showed Hazel that hollow in the tree. She didn't remove the robin's egg. The sun bleached it and the elements weathered it, but it stayed safely tucked away from the wind. She knew he would come back for it someday.

Six months later she checked the spot and it was gone. She had spent the day wondering if Charlie had returned.

"Where did you go?" Ellie asked. "I mean – where did you move to? I didn't even know you were going to be gone!"

"Neither did I," said Charlie, running his hands through his hair. "One day the movers came, and my mom said we needed to go be with family in Ohio." He playfully pushed her shoulder back. "Hey, I thought you had moved first. I saw you and your family load up all of this stuff in your truck and drive away, and you were gone for a couple days. When my mom said it was time to go, I guess I figured everybody was moving on." He followed Ellie over to a fallen log and they sat down together. "Where did you go?"

"Oh, just, like, on a trip or something. I don't remember." Ellie squirmed a little, thinking of when they first took furnishings to the berm house just across the river, up the embankment and across the small valley, less than fifteen minutes away from where they now stood. "But, wait – why are you back? I mean…are you back? Like, *back* back?"

"For now, yeah. My aunt died. Back in Ohio."

"Oh. I'm so sorry."

"It's okay. She was nice, but her house smelled like beef."

"Beef? And that was a bad thing?"

"Well, when it's beef that still smells like the barnyard, then yes. It was a very bad thing."

Elli laughed. "And that's where you lived? With your aunt?"

Charlie nodded, reaching down to pull on some grass peeking out of the forest floor. "Yeah."

"And now you're back at your old house?"

"Yeah. Weird, right?"

"Mm – hm. So crazy."

They remained for a minute in silence. Ellie couldn't help noticing the rhythm of his breathing and hoped he could not tell that she had purposefully matched her rhythm to his. Around them the forest continued its happy existence with no thought of them whatsoever. The birds chirped. The water gurgled and flowed. The trees spread their leaves to catch the sun and soaked up nutrients from the earth. A squirrel chattered away high in the fir trees, chastising a foe.

"How often do you come out here?" Charlie broke the silence, turning his body toward her.

Ellie shrugged. "I don't know. Probably a couple times a week."

Charlie nodded, thinking. "Doing home school?"

"Yes," Ellie affirmed. "I hate it, so I am getting it done as soon as possible. I only have seven more classes or so before I can take the test. You?"

Charlie's eyes grew a little distant. "I'm joining the ARC community engagement team."

Ellie's heart sank. That meant he would be travelling most of the time. "Oh. When? I mean...how long do you..."

"Have until I go? Two weeks. Then I am off to training. I mean, it's still here in town, but...yeah. You can't really leave or anything."

Ellie nodded. "Do you actually want to join?"

He stood with an enthusiastic energy and breathed deeply. "Yeah. I do. I just don't know if I want it to start so fast. But," he said, reaching back down to pick up his pole and tackle box, "this is part of growing up, I guess." He gestured with his head up the river. "I'm going around the bend to fish. Want to join?"

She did. More than anything she wanted to join. She stood and smoothed her jeans and dropped the pinecone she had been picking at with her hands. Ellie knew she needed to get back home, to check on mother, to try and make things right again between them. She couldn't leave her all alone today.

"I better head back home," she said reluctantly.

"Okay," Charlie said. He averted his eyes and then returned his gaze. "I'm not sure my mom would want me to...well.." He trailed off, trying to find a kinder way to say *Mother doesn't want me to talk to you.*

Ellie held up her hand, understanding. "It's okay. My mom...well, things are different. Than they were."

Charlie gave a little tweak of his mouth and a single, affirming nod, searching her face for what "different" meant. Finding nothing, he said. "Yep. Welp. Okay."

Ellie held her hands awkwardly in front of herself. "I'm glad we found each other – like, just, randomly out here. That was weird."

He shot her a strange look.

"But cool! I mean. How cool is this?" She felt like someone else had taken over her mouth and was causing words to spill out that were not at all what she wanted to say. She tried to save herself from total embarrassment by starting to walk away. She knew she would need to pretend to head back to the farmhouse so that he wouldn't see her going toward the berm house. She walked slowly and deliberately, hoping he would round the bend quickly so she could turn around and hop across the creek.

"See you soon sometime," he called out.

Ellie smiled and waved. Years later, he really had returned – and Ellie's heart felt like a robin's fragile eggshell, split open with the cupped expectation of being found.

iv

when a sponge is filled

it expands

it takes on more

and more water

and in so doing

it grows

the seed follows suit

becoming heavier

brighter

no eyes to appreciate

the concealed wardrobe

cells bursting with

Charlie-horse pains

molecules expanding and contracting

with the rapid onset

of *becoming*

and all that remains

is to surrender to the burgeoning chaos

and grow

and breathe

knowing that in the end

hurting increases yield

CHAPTER 5

Later that evening, once Mother had gathered the cats and spoken to the moon, Ellie settled her into bed and found herself drawn to the family room couch, emotionally exhausted. The events of the day washed over her consciousness and led her nowhere in particular. Ellie's hurried trek home. Her mother's clean, washed appearance when she first had arrived that morning. The comforting kitchen smells. The fight. The boy. Charlie. *Charlie.* Once her mind had traveled to handsome boy territory it became hard to think of anything else. She searched the room for a distraction.

Ellie picked up the copy of *The Seed Garden* and began leafing through the familiar pages. *Taxonomy and Nomenclature, Pollination Methods, Timing the Harvest, Drying Seeds for Storage.*

Ellie had repeatedly devoured every word, picture and illustration from the time she was very little. Copies of this book were very rare now, and father had said theirs would probably be worth a lot of money had they not marked it up with notes. *Many of these varieties don't even exist anymore, Ellie.*

She could identify most plants and their seeds by sight. She had spent her childhood counting shriveled, dried peas into her palms, filling gossamer bags, and labeling them by her father's side.

"These peas are the same that were grown by Thomas Jefferson. He and his neighbors had a contest to see who could get a bowl of peas to the dinner table the quickest each spring," he would say as Ellie scrawled *Early Frame Peas* on the dangling tag. On the other side, *55 days.* "These are special," he often said. "Not many people have these."

Ellie remembered the sight of him during seed saving season surrounded by his bins and envelopes and bags and notes, a king in his kingdom, a servant to his master, an accountant of all that mattered. It wasn't until just a few months before he was gone that saving seed for food crops was upheld as illegal across the board by the Supreme Court for both farmer and gardener alike.

Father had been very quiet that day.

Mother's favorites had always been the things that were continuously growing or came back on their own year after year – "perennials" in garden speak. The apple trees, the grapevines, the asparagus. *Mother Nature is so generous.* Ellie would help her gather the tender green spears in April from the sandy soil down by the riverbank, her cotton apron held out like a hammock, her sharpened knife slicing through the stalks with ease. Ellie had brought some of their farmhouse asparagus patch to the berm house last fall. She fortified the boggy soil by mixing in some sand. The effort had been a gift for her mother's birthday in October. When she had held her hand and led her to the patch, her mother's eyes danced when she saw the prepared earth. She sensed what it meant.

"Next year?" she had asked.

"Next year," Ellie answered.

It was nearly April already and the small orchard out back was budding and blooming with reckless abandon despite its young age and the long, cold winter. The trees were only five or six years old, having been started in pots by Mother a few years before moving to the berm house.

They had a cherry tree, perhaps Ellie's very favorite, bearing fruit of the Rainier variety. It was a beautiful cherry, red and yellow and sweet beyond description. They had an Asian pear, a White Nectar and Elberta peach, and one each of Aurora Golden Gala, Golden Russet, and Rome Beauty apples, which were Father's favorite.

Mara had an affinity for the grapes, and she enjoyed spending long hours pruning and training the vineyard back at the farmhouse. The white Himrods and dark Concords stood in beautiful contrast to one another in the golden fall sunshine. Ellie had brought Mara a big, hidden bag of each kind to the ARC for the last two harvests. Technically this was fine, as grapevines were a perennial that didn't require seed saving to produce, though one definitely could save seed to preserve the variety if seeds were present, and this fact made local growers reluctant to put themselves in the spotlight. Ellie always made the argument that the varieties they grew were seedless. Mara would protest and glance nervously around, but she always took them. Ellie would wait until the latter half of the walk back to the berm house to bring out her own bag of the Concords to snack on, as then it did not matter if the powerfully purple juice spilled down her chin and onto her shirt. Sometimes she liked to take handfuls of them, sun-warmed and full to bursting, and delight in the visceral experience of squishing them full force in her fists, the grape guts streaming in royal rivulets down her forearms, staining her with the wealth of earth's abundance, making her sticky, and sweet, and in great need of a bath.

Ellie looked at the notes scribbled in her father's unmistakable handwriting down the margins of most pages of the book. This book was, in essence, their family bible. It stayed in the center of their gathering space, year after year. Their names and achievements were scrawled in the pages – *Mara's record pumpkin 65 ½"* – and instead of birth dates or christening dates, tiny planting dates were listed in the back cover for easy reference, with extra pages taped in whenever they ran out of room. Their weekly Sunday meetings more often than not included a gardening calendar check-in along with the customary hymns and prayer. *We are not gardeners of food. We are not gardeners of flowers. We are seed gardeners, seed farmers. Protectors of life.*

Thinking of the gardening calendar brought Ellie to her feet, and she approached the large bookshelves, scanning the end of the third shelf on the right. It wasn't where they normally kept it, and Ellie felt awful for neglecting it for so long. Where had it gone? Many gardening chores had gone by the wayside under her stead, but she could hardly have done them all on her own. She felt a pull to get back to the earth and reconnect with her father in the dirt, reclaim the only thing that made sense to her in this world – growing things.

She made her way back into the kitchen, thinking that maybe the calendar had been absent-mindedly stashed with the cookbooks. As she entered the room she could see that her mother's bedroom door was ajar.

Her bedside lamp cast a warm glow across the empty bed. It was the fairy lamp that Ellie and Mara had given her for Mothers Day many years prior when the girls were still of the age when fairies are of supreme interest.

It was a woodland fairy lamp, and the base of it was the sculpted trunk of a tree, gnarled and full of character. A friendly blue-green door with wrought iron scrollwork stood carved into the roots, complete with a peek-a-boo window and welcome mat. The lampshade was made of the branches with dangling leaves of glass, and when lit it had a magical, sparkling quality.

Ellie had spent many afternoons waiting for the sun to go down just enough so that she could look into the tiny window on the door and see inside when she turned it on. Try as she might during the daytime, the sunlight from her mother's bedroom window and skylight wouldn't allow her to peer past the reflective glare to the miniature world held inside.

One afternoon when she couldn't bear the wait, she had carried the lamp into her closet, plugged it into an extension cord, and gently touched the base to illuminate it. Her eyes danced about, creating stories about the fairies who lived there, peeking inside to see the staircase winding up, a little bookcase, and a table and chair.

She had wished to be able to shrink herself enough to enter and climb those stairs to see where they lead, to take those tiny books off of the shelf and see what stories they held.

She had been too young to appreciate that sometimes not knowing is a gift.

The staircase ending in a lightbulb socket and the fake books cemented in with illegible titles scribbled down the spine wouldn't hold a candle to the magical attic and fantastical tales her imagination supplied her with.

Ellie's eyes moved from the lamp to the bed – *empty. Where is she?* Ellie hadn't seen her mother come out of her room, and there wasn't an external door at that end of the house. Was she in the bathroom? The hallway door to the only bathroom was open just as Ellie had left it, with no one inside. Ellie started to wonder if she was dreaming, if she had fallen asleep on the couch leafing through the seed bible.

Her parent's room did not have a closet to speak of, but her father had made a big, built-in cabinet along the back wall. It was beautifully made, with nice pine wood that had been stained dark and varnished to perfection. There were two sets of double doors that opened up, a side-by-side, his-and-hers kind of thing. The inside of the wardrobe was deep and spacious.

After her father had put the main frame together, Ellie remembered her mother seeing it for the first time. Her eyes lit up and she smiled, putting her arms around him.

"Oh, my goodness, this is huge inside!" she laughed. Then, quietly, "It's so big you could probably…"

Her father had lifted his finger to her lips, nodding in Ellie's direction and pulling her even closer to him, burying his face in her neck.

"Lynnie-loo, I love you," he had whispered.

Ellie could see that the left-hand side of the cabinet was open, with her father's clothing pushed apart in the middle. She could hear rustling and her mother's voice. "Where is it? I swear it was...you'd think I'd never even lived here..."

"Mom?" Ellie called out nervously. "Mom, you okay?" She couldn't understand why the sound was coming from the clothing. Why was her mother in the cabinet?

Suddenly, her mother's voice – *a-ha!* – and then light came flooding out of the cabinet into the room.

Ellie came to stand in front and was very surprised to find her mother behind the clothing standing in the entrance to a long, narrow room that seemed to go on for quite some ways behind her. This part of the house was the back wall that was dug into the earth, and so as far as Ellie had ever known, the wall pushed up against dirt and nothing else. She was both thrilled and bewildered that her home actually held spaces she had never explored. It also felt a bit sad, like a secret had been kept from her – because it *had* been kept from her.

"Mom? What is this?!" Ellie stepped through the clothing and found her footing on the concrete, her words flustered and her cheeks hot. Inside the space there were lightbulbs strung along the center of the ceiling. The wires were suspended between them by cup hooks. On both sides of the room were shelves upon shelves built from weathered pallet wood but still of solid construction. The shelves went from floor to ceiling and were maybe two feet deep. Her mother was motioning for Ellie to follow her.

She walked in the five-foot walkway to the back of the room, maybe fifteen feet, and then was surprised to see her mother turn and continue to the right. Ellie's jaw dropped as they serpentined back and forth across what must have been the full width of their home.

The endless shelves were populated with an assortment of repurposed boxes, most of them skinny and long and shallow. Here an old tuna can box, there a shoebox. The boxes were open on the top and were filled with small envelopes and stapled paper bags.

We are not growers of food. We are seed farmers, Ellie. Brassica napus. Helianthus tuberosus. Pastinaca sativa. Solanum lycopersicum.

Her father's voice sang from the shelf labels through the old Latin words she hadn't heard since the day he was gone. She found herself in the midst of them aching to resurrect him with letters, hold him with nomenclature, find him again between the paper bags and contraband dusty hulls. He was a rebel, her father. She felt proud.

Ellie followed her mother to the very last shelves, the only ones made of metal, where she was pulling out a bigger box from toward the bottom labeled *RESEARCH*. She smiled as she hefted it up, and Ellie ran to help hold it.

"Oomph! It's heavier than I remember!" her mother said. "Help me get it out to the table."

She was acting completely normal again. Well, "normal" given the context of a hidden room full of seeds and a mysterious box. Ellie was going to observe and listen and try to piece together as much as she could without breaking the spell that her mother seemed to be under. Ellie was hungry for her mother.

They shuffled through the serpentine layout backwards, sharing the load of the heavy box between them. Ellie ducked her head as they entered into and exited the wardrobe cabinet. Their awkward shuffling ended as they settled a corner of the box on the kitchen table and slid it to the middle.

Her mother sighed. "I don't even know where to begin." She opened the flaps on the top, reaching inside to retrieve a small mountain of papers, pictures, and manila folders. She paused at her next glance into the box and then brought out a nametag. *Dr. Joseph Coleman* it said. *ARC.* She looked at it awhile and then handed it to Ellie. "Criminals. The whole lot of them. Criminals with a smile."

Ellie held her father's nametag in her hands and turned it over and over as she listened to her mother, who had started sorting out the informational mess in piles across the table. The yellow glare of the light hanging above them cast long shadows around the room. Ellie craned to look at the black night beyond the kitchen window and couldn't see anything but a mirrored reflection of her mother's back bent over her work. It was late – just how late was anybody's guess – but her mother was speaking and she was listening, and that was all that mattered in the world, midnight or not.

"Do you know what the last thing I heard your father say was?"

Ellie shook her head no. They had never spoken of that day.

"He was sitting right where you are now before heading to work that day. He looked up from his coffee and he said, 'Remind me to tell you something when I get home tonight.' I asked why he couldn't just tell me right then, and he responded, 'It will ruin the surprise.'"

Ellie remembered her father tousling her hair as he had left for work that day. "See you later, sweet girl," he had said.

Mother slowed her sorting to look Ellie in the eyes. "He always made me promise that I wouldn't tell you or Mara any of these things." She held up some of the papers. "He didn't want you involved."

"Was he in trouble?"

Mother laughed. "Oh, honey. We are *all* in trouble. Most people just don't know it. But your father did. And that…well, they didn't like that."

She handed Ellie a picture of three men and two women standing side by side with lab coats on. The ARC logo was on the wall behind them. One of the men – her father – was shaking hands with another man – Rhett Dixon, Hazel's father. They were smiling at the camera, posing. Upon closer inspection, Ellie recognized the woman as Lydia Dixon, Hazel's mother. The woman standing next to her was wearing a white lab coat and had eyebrows that were quite pronounced.

"When was this?" Ellie asked.

Her mother clicked her tongue while she thought. "Five years ago, maybe? A couple years before ARC first opened in town. I mean, they were already in the planning stages." She pointed at the photo. "This was when Oregon State University gave ARC a huge research grant because of your dad. It took them a lot of persuading to get OSU to consider funding them. Well – until your dad came on board. He was a hot commodity. His brain was, at least. I told him he shouldn't have taken ARC's offer, but he convinced me it was the only way."

"The only way to what?"

Mother smiled and looked down, sighing. She looked up at Ellie. "To get inside." She went back to sorting and Ellie blinked, afraid to push for more information.

"How are you organizing all of this?" Ellie asked.

Her mother's hands went out in a gesture that said *beats me.* "I thought at first I would just sort the photos with photos, papers with papers, but...I don't think that is going to really help us."

"By topic maybe?" Ellie asked, clueless but determined to be useful.

"No," said Mother. "It's all.." she laced her fingers together. "...Interconnected. I would never be able to keep that straight." She tapped her middle finger on her waist, hands on her hips, elbows thrust wide. "We need to go in order." She started undoing all of her work, picking up the piles and putting them back in the box. "This is where your father's undying love for putting a date on absolutely everything in his life will actually come in handy."

Her mother moved the now-full-again box to a chair and grabbed a roll of masking tape out of the kitchen junk drawer. She tore off long strips and used them to criss-cross the surface of the table, creating divided spaces for sorting. She then took a marker and wrote a different year on the tape under each square. "Okay, sweet girl. Let's get to it."

Sweet girl. The words made Ellie's throat get tight and her eyes wet. That is what her father had called her. She blinked and nodded her head.

They each took a handful of stuff from the box, looked for the handwritten date on the top corner or the back or scribbled down the margins, and then placed it in the appropriate square.

Once they got into a rhythm piles were forming fairly quickly, though Ellie or her mother sometimes paused to linger on a picture or to read a caption.

Within an hour Ellie's eyes were starting to droop. Her mother placed her hand on Ellie's shoulder.

"You should get some rest."

"No, it's okay. I want to help."

"It's too much to take on in one night. It will still be here in the morning."

"Will *you* still be here in the morning?" Ellie asked before realizing it.

Her mother pursed her lips but didn't respond. Her eyes were hurt, but they seemed full of compassion, too.

Embarrassed, Ellie put the papers she was holding back into the box and left for her room, mumbling, "Good night," her cheeks blazing.

V

some people seek heat

crowding the cabanas

adoring the desert

loving the absence of snow

allowing the pelting rays into their tanned skin

smiling

some prefer the cold

the very idea of unforgiving sun

causing nausea

you can always get warmer by adding a blanket

they say

but what are you going to do when it's hot

and you've taken off

all your clothes

this seed

is partial to moderate warmth

remaining bundled in cool soil

until the ambience in the air reaches

fifty-five degrees Fahrenheit

on a spring morning

and it takes a sip of water

and it knows

it is time

CHAPTER 6

In the morning Ellie's eyes blinked open to find her mother standing over her. The proximity of another person by her bedside was strange. It had been a couple years since anyone other than herself had been in her room, and her mother's presence caused her to startle and sit up. She bit back the curse words trying to fling themselves from her mouth.

"Holy – what the – Mom. *Mom.*" She covered her eyes with her hands and folded herself over onto her knees.

"I was trying not to wake you too early. It's noon, though, and we need to get going. We won't make it to the farmhouse and back before dark at this rate."

Ellie pulled a sweatshirt over her tank top and knit shorts. "The farmhouse? It's Friday."

"Yes," Mother replied, "and we're already so late." She sat

down on the side of Ellie's bed. "I shouldn't have waited this long to begin with. I'm sorry."

You don't make any sense, Ellie thought. *Where have you been, Mother? Why are you back? When will you go away again?* That's what Ellie and Mara called it – *going away* – when their mother escaped into her mind, freeing herself from responsibility by imprisoning herself mentally.

"It's okay," Ellie said. *Don't leave me.*

The walk to the farmhouse was a dry one. It was that time of March when the sky mimics a high-strung toddler – happy and sunny one hour, angry and crying the next. They were glad of their fortune, as it allowed them to go at a more leisurely pace. Ellie's mother wasn't nearly as strong as she had used to be. The decline in her mind had led to a decline in her muscles and they frequently needed to stop so she could catch her breath.

As they plodded along Ellie thought of the piles left behind on the berm house dining table. She hadn't been able to look closely at much of anything, but what she could piece together was that her dad had known something he shouldn't have, and that something was why he was gone today.

Ellie's memories of her father were mostly positive. He was one of those men who are adorable in a very geeky way. His face was handsome, but his tight auburn curls, large glasses, and lanky limbs worked against any attempt at true coolness. Add being a scientist to the mix and the poor guy truly had no chance – but, he truly didn't care, and that is what made him the most cool of all.

Ellie's friends knew they could count on Dr. Coleman to remember their actual name and then give them a new 'scientific' name. "Ah, it's Hazel Dixon! Or, as I like to call her, *Hazelous magnificum.*" It was a dad joke of horrific proportions that embarrassed Ellie to no end yet truly delighted her friends. One year she had made him a Father's Day card wherein she scrawled in her best 10-year-old cursive *Fatherus Fantasticus.* He pulled her up on his lap and made no mention of her blunder in capitalizing the second word of a scientific name. "I love it," he whispered.

When he hadn't come home that first evening their mother sat in her room near the window on a chair she had dragged in from the kitchen. That had been the beginning of her going away. She had made his favorite dinner that night – lasagna.

She was excited to hear whatever news he had promised to share earlier that morning and making lasagna was her way of contributing to the occasion. After the sun went down and he still wasn't home, mother wrapped his portion and placed it in the refrigerator, still on their nice china and ready to be reheated at a moment's notice.

Ellie still remembers that lasagna waiting in the fridge for months, growing first white and then blue and black with mold. Mara was the one who had to finally throw it away. Mother had cried and cried.

Ellie had nearly thrown up when she came across the yucky pile in the wild grass beside the berm house.

It took the critters less than twenty-four hours to make her father disappear for good.

Her mother struggled to get up the sharp embankment on the other side of the river as they neared the farmhouse property. Ellie showed her the best footholds and where to hang on to branches, patiently holding out her hands as supports and talking her through it. Her mother smiled as though things were okay, but Ellie could tell that the trip was truly taking its toll on her. What normally took Ellie one hour to walk took the two of them nearly three. Ellie wished they had brought some extra snacks along. She only had a sip of water left in her canteen. She knew that her mother had grown weaker, but how much so became very apparent on that day. Her mother knew it as well. Ellie could see it in her eyes.

They finally made it to the crest behind their pasture and barn where they paused to rest and look out on the peaceful scene. Her mother breathed in and put her hand up to her heart as she gazed.

"Oh, Ellie," she said. "We're home."

She hadn't seen their in-town property for two years.

That evening was spent getting Ellie's mother to eat something and to go to bed early. Ellie got a jar of broth and canned chicken and fashioned a soup with some of the ARC dried noodles and canned vegetables.

She tried to ignore the pull of her phone as it charged. Every few seconds it vibrated with the delayed reception of text messages and alerts, probably from Hazel. Each time the screen lit up Ellie would look toward it and then away, focusing on her mother and the task at hand. *I can look at it when she's asleep,* she told herself.

She had been relieved to find the power on when they arrived and was glad to know where the fuse box was, thanks to David.

She didn't mention any of that to her mother.

After dinner she helped her mother up the stairs despite protests that help wasn't needed. "I just wanted to get a few things and go back home tonight." Ellie told her staying the night was a better idea as they walked down the upstairs hallway to the room that her parents had slept in. As she pushed open the door to the dismally dusty bedroom Ellie wished she had taken it upon herself to clean the other rooms more regularly – and by regularly, she meant *ever*. The evening sunlight streamed in through the front-facing window. The cloud of dust that was kicked up by the movement of air swirled in the light, thick and cough-inducing. Her mother looked back at Ellie, one eyebrow raised. "Guess I'm sharing with you?"

By the time Ellie had gotten her mother into a nightgown and ready for bed she found herself equally exhausted. Even the thought of her buzzing, fully-charged phone downstairs wasn't enough to pull her from the call of a soft pillow and comfortable bed.

She climbed in next to her already sleeping mother and pulled up the quilt that Ellie had made by hand, under her mother's tutelage. *This square came from my Easter dress. This rosebud, my grandmother's handkerchief.* She felt the soft, worn cotton under her fingers, running them along the two lines of stitching, her mother's and her own, side by side around the perimeter. One line of stitches was straight and even, consistent, practiced; the other grew better in fits, here too long, here too short, here a mishmash of both. By the time they had made it around the entire quilt the stitches were nearly identical.

"It only takes one quilt," her mother had said. "You're a real professional now."

Now, laying by her mother's side, Ellie remembered how it had felt to crawl under that quilt for the first time, to wrap herself in something of her own creation that was filled with tangible evidence of love and memories past.

Ellie studied the rise and fall of her mother's chest, the line of her nose, the delicate way her dark eyelashes curved against her pretty face. She carefully reached out to touch her shoulder, her hands. They were always so soft. The moon was glowing through the window and Ellie's eyes followed the curve of light to the vault of her ceiling where one wood beam ran perpendicular to the window. The snowflakes she had made as a young girl were still pinned with strings to the wood above her. She gazed at the designs, doing her best to make out the roughly cut stars and hearts and unnamed shapes in the moonlight. Though they were childish and not impressive, she still felt that seven-year-old pride every time she looked at them.

It didn't take long for Ellie to join her mother in sleep, and the dreams that followed were full of disjointed images and locations. She spent the night trying to find her shoes in the woods or trying to remember her name in a crowd of strangers. She dreamed of the message tree and of desperately trying to get outside to check for a note from Charlie, unable to find the door in an unfamiliar building that was also somehow her house. Images of her father would float through every now and then, along with words that had stood out from the piles in the kitchen. *Fraud. Scientist.*

Whistle-blower. Fake.

In the morning Ellie woke to an empty spot where her mother had been. She stretched and rubbed the sleep from her eyes, turning on her side for one last minute of snoozing. She grabbed her second pillow and hugged it in front of her, ready to slip back into unconsciousness when her mind asked the question *where did she go? Is she safe?* and Ellie couldn't ignore the tug of love and responsibility.

She sat up and then stood beside the bed, getting her bearings. She could hear a sound of wood scraping on wood somewhere in the house. She shuffled out of the bedroom into the hallway and let her ears guide her to her dad's old office on the back of the house, above the kitchen. There she found her mother, still in her nightgown, attempting to pull his behemoth of a desk out from the wall.

"Mom? What are you doing?"

"What I should have done last night. Here, help me."

Ellie grabbed hold of the corners on one side while her mother grabbed the others. Inch by inch they scooted the massive piece of hand-carved furniture out into the room a couple of feet. They wiped the dust from their hands when there came a knock at the door, quick and nervous. Ellie was used to ignoring knocks at the door while at the farmhouse, so she shrugged and asked, "What are we looking for?"

Her mother pointed toward the front door. "You're not going to get that?"

Ellie looked down at her gauzy nightgown and imagined the state of her wild, curly hair. "Mom!"

"Ellie, we can't let them think we aren't here."

"Them?"

"Just go see who it is. Please? Look through the peephole, at least."

Ellie skittered her way downstairs, avoiding the creaky treads in the stairway. She pushed her eye up against the peephole as she stood on tiptoe. Outside she could make out the form of Hazel, looking worried and pacing back and forth. She opened the door with a spurted "Boo!" which made Hazel jump and curse at Ellie, who was laughing.

"Shut up, Ellie. It's not funny."

"Why are you here?"

"Why are you feeling so normal right now? Did you not see?"

Ellie stopped smiling. "See what?"

"Where's your phone?" Hazel pushed past her into the house, looking around.

Ellie pointed to the armchair. "It's over there. Charging. What are you talking about, Hazel? What happened?"

Hazel grabbed Ellie's phone, held it up to Ellie's face to unlock it, and tapped away while she talked. "The world is freaking crazy right now, okay? You just seem to not always…know what is going on, so I wanted to come make sure."

Ellie looked out the window. "Did you walk here?"

Hazel tapped one last time at Ellie's phone and then held it up to her. "Just watch."

A video was playing. It seemed to be a compilation of clips with protestors holding signs that said things like *You Aren't God* and *Nature is King* standing next to one burning building after another. A newscaster's voice was dubbed over the footage.

"Protestors took to the streets today in eleven Oregon cities within three different counties, targeting seed banks and warehouses with fire. The protestors say they feel compelled to reverse the damage done by the Agricultural Research Corporation and its subsidiaries, saying, quote: 'God is the great Creator. You are the great destroyer.' – end quote. The damage comes right before the planting season here in the Pacific Northwest and poses an imminent threat to food security within the state of Oregon. We can expect food supplies to be shorter and food production to take longer – or halt altogether for some Oregon facilities – in the coming months as Oregon's current stores of grain get depleted. For now, citizens are urged to stay calm and wait for a full accounting of the damage while the USDA, Oregon Dept. of Agriculture, and the Coalition for Food Security discuss the best plan of action moving forward. Rhett and Lydia Dixon, the husband-wife leadership team at ARC, could not be reached. When asked of the possibility of securing seed from federal reserves, the USDA had no comment at this time. The governor wants the people of Oregon to be assured that their first priority is to take care of the citizens' needs."

Ellie stared in horror at the screen as it showed footage of a building at ARC blazing high into the sky. "Oh, my – my sister!" Ellie took her phone from Hazel and walked to the kitchen, trying to make sense of what she just saw. She sat down at the table and Hazel joined her.

"Nobody was hurt," Hazel said. "It was just a warehouse that was rarely used, luckily. Your sister is okay."

Ellie breathed out and relaxed. "So...people are burning seeds?" If no one could save seeds, didn't that mean that there were less of them to go around? "Why would they do that?"

"Not just any seeds. ARC's seeds. My parents' seeds...what if they had been at work that night? Sometimes they have to go to the warehouse after hours to do…I don't know, stuff. They could have died."

It was now that Ellie noticed the text messaging bubble with 21 notifications. "Oh, Hazel, I am so sorry. I was so tired last night, I just went to bed early." She wrapped her friend up in an awkward across-the-table hug. "I had no idea anyone was upset about ARC."

Criminals. The whole lot of them. Criminals with a smile, her mother had said.

"I thought it was supposed to be the best thing ever, 'the new way.' Mara sure seems to think so," said Ellie.

"Well, there are people against it. Against progress, I guess. Want to stick to the old way of doing things. And they're willing to burn it to the ground to prove it."

Hazel paused.

"That's not all that's going on, Ellie. I heard…" she hesitated.

"Heard what?"

"I heard them talking. About you."

"Me? Who is 'them'?"

"My parents. And Sheriff Jack. At my house last night."

Ellie glanced over Hazel's shoulder at the stairway, wondering if her mother was listening. "Oh? Saying what?"

"Well, at first he was just asking them questions about the fires and anyone they knew who might be involved. Their voices got lower and I could hear something like 'who knows what's going on there.' Then they saw me listening. Sheriff Jack smiled and pointed at me, saying 'This young lady can probably answer our question.' And then they all smiled at me, real weird, and then my mom said, 'How is Ellie, honey? Is she doing well?' And I said, 'uh, yeah, I guess. I just saw her a couple days ago.' And they said, 'And her mom?' and I didn't know what to say, 'cause I, you know, haven't seen her in a long time and whatever. But I just said, 'yeah, she is doing okay.' And Sheriff said 'You've seen her?' And I said, 'Well, no…but Ellie is taking care of her and says she is okay.' And then they all looked at each other and nodded but they were quiet and weird, and then my mom told me to go get ready for bed."

Hazel leaned across the table and got a very serious look in her eyes. "I will always be your friend, but I need you to tell me the truth." Her face began to grow red. "Ellie?" She placed her hands flat in front of her. "Did you kill your mother?"

Ellie blinked in disbelief.

Hazel didn't budge, determined to receive an answer. Ellie fumbled for words, not willing to accept that her friend suspected her of murder.

"No she didn't – but she nearly scares me to death when she stays too late at your house, sometimes."

Hazel whirled around to see Ellie's mom smiling on the staircase. She had gotten dressed in some navy knit pants and a gray cable knit sweater and had pulled her hair back into a neat bun. She looked somewhat frail, but definitely not dead, and the red in Hazel's cheeks deepened to a crimson as she stammered out an apology, not knowing whom to apologize to first.

"Oh, my god. Ellie. Mrs. Coleman. Oh, my god. I am so sorry. I..." She covered her face with her hands.

Ellie laughed despite the hurt that was inside.

Hazel thinks I could do that? <u>Would</u> do that?

Ellie thought back to her interactions with Sheriff Jack at the ARC two days prior and could see that he had been feeling her out.

Did they really suspect her of murder? Or did they just think her mother was dead?

Ellie's mom descended the remaining steps and laughed, putting her hands on Hazel's shoulders. "It's okay, Hazel. I have been a bit of a recluse for a while. It is true. If anything, it is good to know people care about me." She reached over to stroke Ellie's cheek. "This one could never harm a fly. She's too good inside."

She walked over to the shelf above the stove to grab the teapot. "Besides," she said, tapping her finger on Ellie's phone as she went to fill it with water in the sink, "She knows no mom equals no money for a phone." She winked at her daughter. "I mean, one has to think about the consequences of one's actions."

"Yeah, thanks," said Ellie. She couldn't look Hazel in the eye.

Hazel took the hint.

"I think I am going to go."

"So soon?" Ellie's mom pointed at the teapot. "Only takes a minute."

"No thanks, Mrs. Coleman. I better get home." Hazel turned to Ellie. "Just…keep your phone on, okay? I might…need you. Or something."

"Yeah." It was Ellie's cheeks that were burning now. "I'm glad your family's okay."

It seemed like an eternity as Hazel collected her things and let herself out the front door. Ellie and her mother stayed quiet for a long time afterwards. Ellie wasn't sure if her mother had heard what had happened at ARC or not, and if not, she wasn't so sure she wanted to tell her.

Her mother drank her tea and Ellie made some toast, running upstairs to get dressed before the bread popped up, ready to be buttered and slathered with jam. *I'll take a shower tonight,* she told herself when she sniffed her armpits before pulling a shirt over her head. *Right now there is too much to do.*

But what was there to do? Ellie had no idea. She didn't know why they had come to the farmhouse.

She was trying to be so careful when it came to her mother's state of mind. One tiny misstep could make her go away again, and Ellie was enjoying the sound of her voice and the sight of her smile.

Ellie chomped on her toast while her ears bathed in her mother's humming as she was washing her tea mug. Her mind replayed the footage Hazel had showed her. *Why are people burning the seeds?* she wondered. *What's so bad about them?* Of all the information she had gleaned from Mara and from the literature put out by ARC at the library, they were changing the world of food production for the better. *Feeding You Feeds Us. Local produce. Organic. Training the Next Generation of Harvesters.* Ellie knew that her mother was not fond of them, and that her father had worked for them, but neither of those facts explained anything about the current situation.

The sound of another knock came as Ellie was brushing the final crumbs from her mouth, this time louder and more confident. They both looked toward the front door. Ellie swallowed the last bite of toast and jumped up. "It's probably Hazel again. Maybe she forgot something."

Ellie didn't bother to check the peephole this time as she yanked the door open. She about jumped out of her skin when she saw Sheriff Jack standing there in full uniform. "Oh! My...you scared me!"

He looked comically to his left and right as though he was trying to figure out the cause of her alarm. "Did you see a monster, or something?"

Ellie shook her head, trying to act normal and smile. "No. I just...wasn't expecting you, I guess."

She wasn't sure if she should trust him – but then again, who could blame him? It was his job to be aware of his community and enforce the law. The previous couple of years Ellie *had* been acting strange and her mother *had* been absent. Probably anyone with half of a mind would have come to the same conclusion, or at least considered the possibility of foul play. He cared about their family, or at least she thought that he did. They had been friends for what seemed like forever.

Sheriff, who had never married, was like a part of their family. He spent every holiday at their house until her father...died? Disappeared? Ran away? Was killed? They had never gotten any answers.

Ellie started to relax her stance on the doorstep.

"Is that Jack?" Ellie's mother's voice rang out behind her as she approached the door.

Sheriff Jack's face seemed to melt in a surprised giddiness. "Oh, my God! Evy?"

Ellie could feel the energy between old friends and stepped to the side, watching their reunion with trepidation and curiosity. Jack wrapped his arms around her mother and held her close.

Extremely close.

"You're...how are you? My God, Evelyn - I haven't seen you or heard from you –"

" – I know, I know. I've been giving everyone a good scare." They separated and took a step back to look at each other.

"Every time I come by there's usually no answer. I was starting to think...well, a lot of things."

"I don't blame you, Jack. I just...I needed time, I guess. Still do."

They both looked sideways at Ellie who was lingering and listening in.

"Ellie, honey – why don't you go finish cleaning up in the

kitchen?"

Ellie looked from her mother to Jack and back again. "Okay," she said. "Good to see you, Jack."

"Good to see you, too, Ells Bells."

Ellie went to the kitchen and began putting things away, making sure to make some noise. Once they were satisfied that she wasn't listening they switched from polite talk to things more personal. Ellie tried to listen in between her carefully placed cupboard door closings and plate shuffling.

"Nothing? Still nothing?" Ellie could hear the sound of her mother's hands slapping down against her thighs with exasperation.

"Evy." There was a warmth that Ellie did not like. "We're trying. But it truly is like he vanished. It haunts me every night, Evy, it really does."

"Hmm."

Ellie could hear disbelief in her mother's voice. *I don't believe him either, Mother.*

"Evy. Don't do this."

Ellie looked up to see the reflection of the two of them in the hallway mirror. Jack was reaching out to take Evelyn's hand. She withdrew it.

"No."

Jack shifted his weight. "At least let me get a phone line going again. I worry that if something happened you wouldn't be able to call for help."

"What's going to happen, Jack?"

His eyebrows knit together. "Well, anything *could* happen. Accidents do happen, you know." He put his hands on his hips. "Why are you being like this?"

"Eliyah has a cell phone. We'll be fine."

He shuffled his feet. "What if I wanted to call you?"

Evelyn grabbed the door handle. "Find my husband," she said, gesturing for him to leave and then closing him out from her presence once he reluctantly stepped across the doorframe.

Ellie had come out of the kitchen and stood in the hallway. Evelyn leaned her head on the back of the door and took a few big breaths before turning around. When she saw Ellie, she started.

"Oh! Baby. You scared me."

She looked over her shoulder to watch Jack through the window as he got into his truck and drove away. "They suspect something. I can tell. We'll need to stay here for a while." She looked back at Ellie with sadness in her eyes. "I'm sorry for all this,

Ellie."

Ellie blinked away the tears that started stinging at her eyes. She wanted to hear the apology, to hear that her mother understood all she had done for her the last two years. All of the going back and forth, keeping up the pretense though it made absolutely no sense to her. All of the housework, though imperfect. All of the yardwork, and gardening, though certainly scaled back and lacking. All of the cooking, the taking care of the chickens.

At the same time, Ellie could suddenly see her mother more clearly. She saw a woman who had been robbed by grief. A woman who had sat at the windows of her room and of her mind, waiting for a sign of the man she loved to come and make time start ticking again. It all had been a massive pause for Evelyn, one huge heartbeat, a reckoning between hope and reality that, for her, had been instantaneous, but for Ellie, years in the making.

Ellie came to her mother and gave her a hug. "It's okay, Mom." *It's not okay. Please let it be okay.*

Evelyn hugged her back with a fierce tenderness.

Over her mother's shoulder Ellie could see someone walking to the edge of their property. Through the grimy windows she could tell that it was Charlie.

He was heading for their message tree. She saw him place

something in the secret spot, think better of it, remove it, walk away a few feet only to turn back around and again deposit it in the tree. He looked toward their house, and then his own, and started back for his front door, glancing back over his shoulder every five seconds or so at whatever it was he had left behind. Ellie's heart raced.

She pulled away from her mom and held her by the arms, looking her in the eyes. "I know you were trying to keep me safe from whatever happened. You and Dad, both. But I need to know now. Nothing makes sense. I need you to tell me everything."

vi

the swelling of enzymes

synthesis of proteins

pulsing through the seed

just enough to begin

the machinery needed to build

a living thing

scarcely knowing how

maybe even unaware of

the repairs it is making to its own self

its own flesh simultaneously

familiar and

foreign

the processes are set in motion

following the baton

of an unseen Maestro

keeping time

as it grows

swelling with awe

listening to the music

of miracles

CHAPTER 7

It was late afternoon by the time Ellie found her way out to the tree. She peered down in the sprinkling rain at the special spot, surprised at how much lower it was than she remembered.

We were so small back then.

She found a folded piece of paper under a rock. She smiled and picked both items up, glancing back over her shoulder toward Charlie's house.

She quickly wiped the smile from her face when she saw Charlie's mother coming out of the front door carrying something that looked like a package to be mailed. Her frizzy black hair was partially tamed and pulled to the side in a hasty ponytail. She gave off the air of being hurried and bothered, and Ellie wasn't about to draw any attention to herself. Ellie stashed the rock and note in her coat pocket and quietly retreated back inside.

She stood at the window and watched Charlie's mom pull away in their station wagon, wondering how such a beautiful boy had come from such a harried woman. She hadn't seen his father since their return. Never even asked about him, actually. This realization brought some guilt.

"Checking the mail?" her mother asked from the kitchen. She looked weak and her voice followed suit.

"Mom, why don't you go lay down? It has been a long day already. You're not used to this. You need to rest."

She didn't put up much of a protest. "I suppose. But just a little nap." Her breathing was a little labored on the stairs as she went up. "Don't let me sleep too long," she called out at the top of the landing. Ellie could hear her soft footfall making its way to her bed and the sound of the springs squeaking as she got comfortable.

Ellie's mind wanted to shut down itself after all she had been told that morning. New stories and disturbing facts danced around in her head, colliding against each other as she fought off sleep. The excitement of Charlie's note was the only thread of energy she had left, and the surge of adrenaline in her veins as she retrieved the items from her pocket was noticeable.

Ellie made herself comfortable in the big puffy chair to

examine the goods. The rock was a perfect example of a skipping stone, flat and smooth without any nicks. Their childhood selves would have been fully enamored with its aerodynamic beauty. The corner of her mouth went up in appreciation of this innocent gift. She held it tightly in her palm and then set it to the side.

The note was not folded in any fancy kind of way. Of course, that had always been the pattern – Ellie's notes were often folded into specific shapes and designs, where Charlie's notes were never folded with any kind of thought. Fold in half this way, fold in half the other, without any regard to matching up the corners or making sure the fold was a crisp, perfect edge.

She was glad to see that he was still Charlie.

She paused before opening it. She felt some fear. Nervousness.

What if it said he couldn't talk to her anymore? She wouldn't be able to bear it. She stared at the folded paper for a good five minutes before working up the courage to grab the corners and unwrap the words held inside.

In the center of the paper it simply read:

Hagg Lake 3:00

Dock past the mill

Ellie's heart leapt at the invitation – however cryptic – and then she gasped as she looked up to check the time.

3:15.

No! He'll think I don't care!

Ellie popped up from the chair and tried her best to scurry quietly up the stairs to check on her mother before doing a quick freshen-up in the bathroom. She had her boots and coat back on in record time, stone placed back in her pocket, and all thoughts of taking a nap were now distant history, her new focus being the lake, the time, and a boy.

Ellie half walked, half ran alongside the railroad tracks, knowing that by the time she arrived at the fishing dock her cheeks would be fuchsia from both the effort and the cold. She didn't care, however, if it meant she caught him in time.

She wondered how long he would wait for her before he gave up, and if he did give up, would he head back home along the tracks or follow the creek instead?

Would they miss each other altogether?

Ellie chastised herself for not retrieving the note sooner.

Her boots mashed the gravel and her hood felt extra heavy on her head as she jogged along, so she pulled it back to expose her head and let the light raindrops have their way. It was true that one could usually tell the tourists from the locals in Oregon, though it had been ages since Ellie had been anywhere that tourists were likely to frequent. The way to spot the tourists? Umbrellas.

When she neared the back side of the mill, she retreated from the tracks up into the trees out of habit, not wanting to be seen.

Only one mill worker was out and about as it was nearing the end of the work day. He seemed to be doing last minute tidying and preparations, and his gray canvas coat, dotted with rain, swished as he swung his arms while walking.

Ellie did her best to keep up her speed, but it was difficult in the tree cover without a compacted trail, and she didn't want to bring any attention to herself. As she walked, she watched a large truck with the ARC logo painted on the sides pull around to the back of the mill warehouse.

A couple of men jumped out of the passenger side and spoke to the mill worker who shook his head side to side in response after checking a clipboard. The two men got very close to him, and before Ellie could really make out what was happening, the mill worker was limp and on the ground.

She stopped and blinked her eyes, not sure of what she had just witnessed.

She fumbled with her phone in her pocket, trying her best to pull it out and record without being noticed. She felt her bones melt at the *boop!* her phone emitted when she pressed record. *It wasn't on silent? Ellie! Why didn't I check?*

The men from the truck looked in her direction.

Ellie froze.

Her only hope was that the rainfall was enough to mute the noise and that their look towards her had merely been a coincidence.

Afraid to move, she continued to hold the phone in front of her, still recording.

There's no way they can see me through these trees, right?

She did her best to quell her terrified breathing. Slowly, the men relaxed their vigilant stance and looked away from her general direction and back to the mill worker at their feet.

Together they picked him up and dragged him to the back entrance door, setting him against the building and placing his clipboard in his lap.

They then directed the driver to the farthest bay, guiding the truck to back into the loading dock and then unlocking and lifting the dock gate. The three men then proceeded to lift the back door of the truck and unload what appeared to be filled 25 lb. bags, similar to a large bag of flour or sugar.

She zoomed in with her phone but couldn't really make out any markings or labels of any kind. They used manual forklifts to lift pallets full of the white bags out of the truck and then placed them in the warehouse.

It only took a few minutes for them to complete the task, and almost as soon as they had arrived, they were pulling away.

The mill worker was still unconscious by the back door as their exhaust heaved in his face.

Knowing she could no longer be seen or heard, Ellie stumbled back down to the railroad tracks and commenced running as fast as she could. She had to get to Charlie. Tell him what she saw.

Fast, before he leaves for home!

A couple of times she had to stop and put her head down to catch her breath, hands resting on her thighs. By the time she made it to the fishing dock at the lake she was sure she was quite the sight. Her frizzy hair was half matted down with rain, her cheeks were on fire, and her overall winded frame was anything but attractive as it dragged itself down the incline to the empty floating wood platform.

"Nooooooo," she hissed to herself. Tears formed in her eyes and started to spill down her cheeks, big fat drops that carried with them the weight of everything she had been carrying emotionally.

She did little to quiet herself as she sobbed.

A wave of self-hatred welled up inside. *I mess everything up. I ruin everything.*

She removed the stone that Charlie had given her from her coat pocket and angrily threw it out into the water with no attempt at proper skipping form. It disappeared under the surface with a *ploomp.*

This only made her cry harder.

She sat down on the wood and wrapped herself up into her knees.

She rocked and looked out across the water as she cried.

The lake was beautiful, as always, though choppy in the rain and more gray today as it had no blue sky to reflect. The pine trees on the opposite shore were laden with mist, as if the rows were separated by tufts of carded wool. The air was full of the smells of the forest, earthy and rich. The almost-spring sun was starting its descent in the sky, carrying with it the certainty of dropping temperatures.

Ellie's mind returned to earlier that morning.

"Tell me everything," Ellie had asked of her mother. Her

mother had smiled but her eyes were sad.

"I wish I had told you earlier. I also wish I didn't need to tell you." She reached out to tuck Ellie's hair behind her ear. "Keep you away from all of this."

She motioned with her head towards the staircase, and together they mounted the steps. Her mother led her to her father's office where a small, octagonal wooden box was placed on the desk.

There was a small door in the wall below the window where the desk had been pulled away from. The door was open and a small, old-fashioned key was still turned in the lock. There was just enough space in the wall for that wooden box if it was placed on its end. With the heavy desk and chair in place, the chance of seeing this little door would be almost zero, especially since the outside of the door was fashioned as to blend seamlessly with the wall surrounding it. Only the keyhole would be truly visible, and even that had been painted the same ecru color as the walls.

The wooden box was simple and without carvings, except for some initials in the lower right corner of the lid – M.J.C.

Ellie traced the carving with her fingers. "Dad?" she asked.

Her mother nodded.

His real first name, Morris, was hardly ever mentioned as he detested it. He had gone by his middle name, Joseph, all of his life.

"Have you opened it?"

"No," her mother said, "I waited for you."

Ellie gently lifted the lid. Inside she found some photographs of people she didn't recognize, a small rectangular piece of metal about the size of a military dog tag with some numbers engraved on it, and a handkerchief that was carefully folded as if containing something. Looking up to receive approval to continue, Ellie laid it on the desk and folded back the layers of soft cotton.

There was a small manila envelope, the same kind they used to package their saved seeds. It wasn't sealed, and Ellie carefully lifted the folded over lip to peer inside. She pulled out two small baggies, one with a curl of hair in it, and another with what looked like a piece of blood-soaked gauze.

Ellie put it down, repulsed. The blood was old and dry, a study in oxidized biology. She couldn't help but look back and forth between it and her mother, trying to understand. Her mother was white as a sheet, her eyes blinking, her mouth open.

"What is that, Mom?"

She fumbled for words. "Well, it's…hair and…I think…I am not sure."

"It's blood, Mom. Blood. Why is this in here? Whose is it?"

Her mother shook her head. "I don't know."

"Did Dad ever show this to you before?"

"No. This is the first I've seen it."

"How did you know where to find it?"

"Because he told me."

Ellie was taken back. "You've talked with Dad? You know where he is?" She searched her mother's face for answers. Her mother shook her head and knit her brows together.

"No, no, no. From before. From the night before."

She sank into the large desk chair and looked up at Ellie, going back in her mind to that evening two years prior.

"We had played that game...what is it – that alphabet one – after dinner, remember? And we got things cleaned up and we put you guys to bed and then we went to bed. He held me...he held me so close. He said, 'Evy. I have some things behind my desk. At the farmhouse.'"

She shrugged her shoulders.

"I joked with him, asking if it was a million dollars. He was forever saving things in a drawer, hiding things in a box, making a time capsule, writing list after list and stowing it away. He loved stories of old houses with secret passageways and hidden doors. When we bought this house, I swear it was 95 percent due to there being a small door in the wall."

She smiled and pursed her lips.

"It took him forever to decide what to keep in there. Whenever I asked about it, he would usually just say that he hadn't found the right things yet. And that when he had, he would tell me."

Ellie took out the photographs for a closer look. Even upon further inspection she didn't recognize any of the faces. Stranger still, her father wasn't in them, either. "Do you know who any of these people are?"

Her mother studied the photographs and shook her head. "No. But your dad knew a lot of people." She turned the photographs over to look for dates. "They could be anybody."

"Then what does any of this mean?" said Ellie. She was frustrated. Her tone was more accusatory than she had intended, and she could see the hurt in her mother's eyes.

"Ellie, I don't know much more than you. What I do know is this – your father was very smart, too smart in fact, and somebody didn't like that. He had something, knew something, that he wasn't supposed to know."

"What was it?"

"I don't know exactly. He would never tell me. He didn't want me involved."

She picked up the metal piece and tried to make sense of the numbers: *3627339.* She shook her head, stumped.

"What I do know is that it had to do with ARC, something about the seeds they were developing, and that whatever he knew, he shouldn't share with anyone."

"Is this why people are burning down the seed warehouses?"

"What?" Her mother's eyes looked up at Ellie, searching.

Crap. She hadn't heard.

"Yeah...some people are upset about something at ARC. Don't worry, Mara is okay – but some people burned the warehouse. More than one, actually." For a couple of minutes, Ellie tried to use any of what she knew to mentally connect some dots and came up with nothing. "What are we supposed to do?"

"I don't know. I don't know who to trust. I have been so...gone. From it all." Her eyes were sad and tired. "I'm sorry, Ellie. I'm so sorry."

Ellie gathered her mother up in her arms. "Mom, it's okay. You're here. You're here now." She pulled back to look her in the eyes. "What do you need us to do?"

Her mother's mouth grew into a resolute line and her eyes grew confident as steel.

"We need your father."

The wind from off the lake brought Ellie back to the moment. Missing a boy on a dock was arbitrary. Helping her mother was what mattered now. Ellie took a few final shuddering breaths, shook her arms, and stood up from the platform, being careful to wipe away any splinters or dirt from the backside of her jeans. As she twisted to the right to inspect herself, something to the side of the dock caught her attention. It was a tackle box, left between two rocks on the shore, and a fishing pole propped up beside it. Ellie walked closer and peered down at the box, looking for any markings. There was a strip of masking tape across the upper handle that read *C. Harper.* She smiled a weak smile.

It was going to be hard to fit these items into the tree.

{-------}

By the time Ellie was halfway home she regretted ever deciding to carry back Charlie's things and wondered how he ever stood to carry them that far.

One thought of his strong and muscled arms reminded her that he most likely had an advantage in strength, one that Ellie was loathe to admit. She was strong in her own right and always hated if anyone ever called girls weak on accord of their gender. She had been stronger than many boys in her lifetime and felt it an unfair stereotype. Still, there was no denying that, if put to the test, Charlie's biceps could curl decidedly more weight than Ellie's even with the weekly trips between homes that had toned every inch of her and made her calves like sculpted steel. Charlie's arms and shoulders were thick and solid. Ellie thought about what it had felt like to push against him with her hand the last time they spoke. She wondered how long it would be before she ever felt that again.

Ellie's left foot sank into a small divot in the ground by the tracks, which caused her body to fight to keep its balance. She stopped and spread her arms out, inadvertently knocking the clasp on the tackle box loose, which then opened and began spilling its contents out on the wet and muddy ground.

"Uuuugh," Ellie protested, quickly setting down the box and righting it in an effort to prevent any further purging of hooks and baubles and shiny metal pieces.

She shook her ankle, testing for injury, and was relieved to find herself fully functional.

She dropped to her knees, her cold fingers doing her best to carefully scoop up the tacklebox innards and drop them back in the appropriate places without hooking herself. At first she tried to sort them out neatly, but quickly switched her method to simply getting it housed back in the box, no matter the order, as she truly had no idea what methodology was used in the organizing of such implements.

"I will let Charlie do that for himself," she said out loud, slapping down a gelatinous lure of some kind, slightly resembling a bright orange squid.

"Do what for myself?" a voice ahead of her asked.

Ellie's head snapped up to see Charlie standing about twenty feet away. He had his hands in the pockets of his jeans, and his hooded sweatshirt and Converse sneakers were quite wet from the afternoon's storm. The rain had stopped for a bit now, however, and in the dusky light his smile was the most welcome sight Ellie had ever seen. She pointed to the mess, her heart beating loudly in her chest. "I'm so sorry. My fault."

"Hasn't anyone ever told you it isn't safe to play by the tracks?" he teased, coming to kneel down beside her and help.

"If only I could call this playing," she said, wishing she had a way to check if her tear-stained face had recovered from her long cry yet. "At least now you get to carry it home the rest of the way.

That thing is heavy."

He knit his brows together and sat back to look at her. "This thing?" he smirked.

She quickly corrected her statement. "Well, it's not *that* heavy. For me, anyways. It's just a really long walk, you know. Gets tiring after a while." She didn't like how she felt herself growing feisty but felt helpless to stop it.

"You can switch hands, you know," he said, poking her in the side.

His touch caused a jolt of adrenaline, which unfortunately only encouraged Ellie's mouth.

"Yeah, I know – I'm not stupid."

Charlie grew quiet for a second while Ellie kept piling things into the tackle box, latched it closed, and then stood up again, determined to carry it the rest of the way. "Ellie," he said. "I can carry it."

"Nope. It's all good. I deserve it for…well, you know." Ellie dared to look in his blue eyes. "Sorry I was late."

Charlie nodded. "I got all the way home before I remembered I had left everything." He picked up the fishing pole and started walking alongside her back towards town. "I guess I had other things on my mind."

Me. Say it was me.

Ellie cleared her throat, willing herself to not say anything embarrassing. "We must have passed each other, then. I didn't read your note until it was too late. I came as fast as I could, but – I mean, I understand not waiting around all day for me. Especially in the rain."

"Aw, I don't mind the rain," he said, holding out his free hand like he was catching raindrops. "I guess I just...I don't know." He kicked at a rock or two.

He continued to shuffle along beside her, his facial expressions showing that he was trying to find the right way to say something. "Did you know that my aunt and your dad knew each other?"

"Your aunt? The beef house one? In Ohio?"

"Yeah. Aunt Mabel." Their stride had begun to match each other in rhythm, which was quite a feat for Ellie's short legs. "A few days before she died, I was visiting her in her room. She asked if we would be going back to Oregon, and I told her I didn't know. She said, 'My friend Joseph Coleman lives there.'"

Ellie's eyebrows went up. "Nu-uh. How did she know him?"

"I don't know. Maybe you could ask him?"

"Oh." Ellie realized she hadn't told him yet about her dad.

"After she said that she drifted off and since my mom doesn't like me to talk to you, I didn't dare ask her. But it did get me thinking – is that why she doesn't want me to talk to you? And if so, why?"

"Did your Aunt Mable ever live here?"

"Not that I know of, but her whole life's story I really never cared to know about, you know? And by the time I did, the chemo had made her too weak to tell me."

He slowed and put his hand out to block her from continuing to walk, his palm placed on her stomach, his fingers asking her to turn toward him. Ellie's knees nearly buckled at his touch.

"I just…I was wondering if you would do something with me. For me."

Ellie put down the tacklebox. It was almost dark now and they were nearing the rear of the mill. The mill worker was gone. The security lights sent out their dim yellow glow, and the soft light lit Charlie's face as Ellie turned to face him. His eyes looked serious and his perfect, full lips were drawn together.

"I need your help. And you can totally say no, if you want to."

Ellie did everything she could to prevent her eyes from travelling from his beautiful blue eyes to his soft lips. "What is it?"

"Well, it's the ARC team. I'm, uh…starting my training soon, but they ask every new member to bring another person with them to this meeting thing tomorrow. It's like my first time to show them that I am good at getting people to…you know, to join." His eyes searched Ellie's with trepidation. "I thought of you, and I…well, I don't really know anyone else." His eyes flitted to the side. "Yet."

Ellie could see his hands fingering the side seams of his hoodie as he waited for her response.

"So, you need me to join the community outreach team? Or work at the co-op?"

Charlie's hands came up to gesture she had misunderstood.

"No, no – I mean, unless you *want* to, which would be great – but no, I just have to bring someone along who is a potential recruit. I think we just, I don't know, listen to their whole spiel and I get points for bringing someone and then I fulfilled that requirement and then – yeah. That's all."

The idea of spending more time with Charlie was incredibly welcome, even if it meant going to some boring meeting. Maybe she would even get to see her sister there. Ellie put out her bottom lip, pretending to think about it.

"And what do I get out of it? If I come?"

Charlie's nervous face relaxed into a charming smirk.

"What do you want?"

If only you knew.

Ellie shrugged her shoulders and his hands came out to playfully press them back down.

"I'm sure we can figure out a fair trade," he said, the smile in his eyes causing Ellie's cheeks to blush horribly and her heart to thump in her chest.

The sound of clanging metal rang out behind her. She spun around as Charlie's eyes snapped up to the back of the mill. Every sense on high alert, they searched with their eyes and ears back and forth, but the scene was free of any sign of life. Ellie's heart beat even louder now.

"What was that?" asked Charlie, alarmed.

Ellie suddenly felt as though they were being watched.

"I need to tell you something," she whispered, thinking about what she had seen behind the mill before reaching the dock. "But not here."

IN MY HAND A FOREST

Grabbing the tackle box, Ellie retreated back from the train tracks and up into the trees with Charlie following close behind.

Once they had reached a safe distance, Ellie looked up at the encroaching dark night and thought of her mother, likely sick with worry yet again.

"We need to keep walking."

She glanced over her shoulder through the trees, feeling as though they were being followed.

"I saw something. Earlier."

She picked up her pace.

"Today?" Charlie's long legs had no trouble keeping up with her. He reached out and took the heavy tackle box from her and sternly shook his head when she tried to retain her grasp.

"On my way to the dock. Behind the mill."

"What was it?"

"I don't even know what was happening. First an ARC truck came – well, there was a mill worker back there, like, getting stuff ready for the end of the day or something – and this ARC truck came and two guys hopped out and, I don't know – they didn't kill him – at least I don't think – but then they dragged him over to the door of the mill and backed their truck over to a loading bay and took out a whole bunch of pallet things loaded with big white bags of something."

Charlie tried hard to piece together what she was saying. "It was an ARC truck?"

"Yes. The truck said ARC on the sides."

"What was in the bags?"

"I have no idea. But I recorded it? We can watch it. But not here."

"Did they see you?"

"I don't think so. Even if they did, would they know who I am? I was back in the trees, like this, but the sun was still up, so I guess it is possible. But it was raining." Ellie stopped to think. "Or had the rain stopped?"

"What did they do to him? The mill worker? Did you recognize him?"

"No...but I haven't really...I don't know everyone. Anymore. As much." She fidgeted. "I can't really say what happened for sure. I didn't start recording until after that. The two ARC guys just got really close to him, and then suddenly he was on the ground. There wasn't a gunshot or anything. It was all strangely...quiet, actually. Then they just dragged him over to the door and left him sitting there while they unloaded the stuff."

"Why were you walking so close to the mill on the way back? What if they had still been there?" Charlie said.

"I know. That was stupid." Ellie held some branches out of the way for them to pass by. "I guess I felt bad about being late to the dock, so I wasn't thinking straight. I should have stayed up in the trees."

"Who cares about being late to the dock? Why didn't you say this right when I first ran into you? What if someone saw us together? When we were picking up the stuff from my tackle box?"

"What if they did?"

"I'm just saying, we don't know what any of this means, and now we've gone and gotten ourselves right in the middle of it. We don't know if someone was inside the mill and looking out of the windows."

"At this time of day?"

Ellie stopped walking and turned to face him, taking him by surprise and causing him to bump into her. She tried to be brave while still peering down the pathway behind him.

"I think we might be getting a little bit carried away. I will look at the video, and see what I can find, and probably go show it to Sheriff Jack, and…yeah. That's it. It'll be fine."

"Yeah." Charlie wasn't convinced.

They walked for a long while in silence.

They neared the clearing in the trees that led to the end of the drive where their homes sat, far away from any other houses. The brush was thick here, and one had to be careful to step around the horrible patches of blackberry vines that seemed to overtake every corner of Oregon whenever given the chance. Ellie was thankful for her tall rubber boots and thick jeans.

Charlie wasn't faring so well with his converse sneakers and knit hoodie. Ellie stepped on a few unwieldy vines to allow him to hop over without getting snagged to death by the vicious thorns. They made it back to the northwest edge of Ellie's property with only a few scratches and pokes. Ellie plucked a rogue thorn from the edge of Charlie's hood. Charlie put down his fishing equipment and raked a few pine needles from Ellie's hair. They looked at each other.

"We're like those monkeys that eat each other's lice," Charlie grinned.

Ellie laughed and pushed him.

Those shoulders.

"Why would you say that? Gross."

His hands grabbed her hands as they pushed against his chest. "Careful with the merchandise. You break it, you buy it."

"Well, I don't have any money, so good luck with that."

Charlie let go and ran his hands through his hair. "Tomorrow, I can't really have my mom see me go with…I mean, is there any way I can just meet you there? Like, outside the doors?"

Trying not to be hurt and wondering just what was so horrible about her family that his mom would still object to their interacting after all these years, she looked away and nodded. "At the co-op?"

"Around the back side. There is an auditorium back there, by the north entrance. At ten o'clock."

"Okay."

They stood awkwardly until he gave her a soft punch in the shoulder. "Thanks."

Suddenly unable to think of anything to say, Ellie absent-mindedly patted her pockets as if checking to see she had everything, and then walked toward her front door.

She didn't look back to see Charlie waiting there, watching to make sure she made it safely inside.

vii

treading water

can only be sustained

for so long

legs kicking beneath the surface

energy being extended

with the solid aim of

preserving status quo

the seed can only

tread germination

for so long

mitochondria pulsing in its cells

beneath the surface

beneath the ground

beneath our feet

beneath our consciousness

energy being raked from the

    proteins and

    proteins needing to rake energy

to be synthesized

and so the cycle robs Peter to

pay Paul

but there must be more

there has to be more

the seed knows it is more

than just a

seed

CHAPTER 8

Ellie slipped into the back of the dim auditorium as quietly as she could. Being late to the meeting with Charlie was embarrassing, but the idea of missing it altogether was unbearable, so she made herself follow through. Ellie scanned for a seat that was somewhat close to the aisle. Finding one about five rows down and three seats in, Ellie walked down the aisle and apologized as she began stepping over the occupants of the seats before hers.

It wasn't until she had settled in that she realized Hazel was turning around and smiling at her from the row in front of her. "Ah, a friendly face," she whispered. David nudged her from the side.

"Shh, Hazel." He gave her a very 'older brother' kind of look and then checked up his chin and smiled when the speaker in the front of the room looked in their general direction.

The room was partially filled by about forty people, most of them teens or in their early twenties. It was so quiet and everyone was so attentive that it put Ellie on edge. It had been a long time since she had been in the same room with this many people, and to have everyone so quiet and so focused was a very strange phenomenon to her.

At the front of the small auditorium was a pudgy woman who looked to be in her mid-fifties pacing back and forth as she talked. She was smartly dressed in a long navy skirt and light blue button-down blouse. On the breast pocket there was the logo for the Agriculture Research Corporation, three stalks of wheat embroidered with a golden yellow thread. Her blonde hair was starting to turn gray, and she had it styled in a crown of braids like a German grandmother.

Behind her was a big projection screen that said, "ARC = A Model for the Future." There was an exit door to the left of the small stage that the woman was on, and by that door stood another woman.

It took Ellie a second to recognize that it was her own sister standing there in an ARC uniform. When she came to her weekly co-op shopping day, Mara was usually dressed in the more casual ARC polo shirt with an apron over the top. To see her dressed up and with her hair slicked back into a high, perfect bun was a very new image. She seemed so regal, so grown up. Ellie smiled, hoping to catch her eye, but Mara was entirely focused on the woman speaking to the crowd.

"It is, indeed, very encouraging to see so many young people interested in joining ARC and we want you to know that you are appreciated and very much needed. Here at ARC we are attempting an entirely new model for feeding the world, and it all starts here with our own community. What we accomplish here will greatly impact our ability to grow to other communities, and your efforts are what will help bring that about."

She grabbed a little clicker off of the small table to the right side of the stage and pointed it toward the screen. The slide didn't change.

"What? What am I doing wrong?"

Mara approached her and whispered something while gesturing above the audience's head to the projector.

"Ah! I see. Well, we can't be great at everything, I suppose. Learn something new every day."

"Projectors are new?" Hazel whispered over her shoulder in a sarcastic tone. David poked her again.

The woman pointed the clicker at the projector this time and changed the slide successfully. She looked very pleased with herself. The new slide said: "How Can I Help at ARC?" Underneath the title were three bullet points listing The Farms, The Co-op, and

Community Outreach.

"So," the woman continued. "How can you help here? This is where the fun begins, where we get to know you and your individual strengths. If you had to choose, would you rather work with your hands, organize information and goods, or work with people? Let's take a quick look just to get an idea. How many of you here would most likely want to work with your hands? Working, creating things?"

About twenty people or so raised their hands.

"Don't worry, this isn't locking you into anything," she said to a particularly gaunt looking girl sitting on the front row, who appeared to be afraid of breathing, let alone raising her hand in public. "This is just to get an idea. Okay, so – about twenty or so? And how many would rather organize information and goods?"

David raised his hand and Hazel turned to him, shaking her head. "That's the boring one. Don't choose the boring one."

"Okay, maybe thirty of you…which means, I am guessing, that the remainder of you would prefer to work with people, is that correct?"

Most of the crowd raised their hands for this category, including Hazel. Ellie scanned the room for Charlie. She finally spotted him off to the front left of the auditorium. He wasn't raising his hand. He was looking back directly at her. He smiled and gave a little wave. Ellie gave a small wave in return.

"Ah, yes – to be expected. Most young people do tend to choose working with people, and you are very good at it." She clasped her hands in front of her. "So. Going back to those of you who enjoy working with your hands – you would be best suited working with us on the farm. Let's get a little taste of what that might look like." She pointed to Mara to bring the lights all the way down as she clicked to start a video.

In the video, footage of a lush and beautiful farm operation filled the screen. Young, smiling workers picked corn and laughed as they passed along baskets of apples. A warm female voiceover talking about "returning to the earth," "earth-centered values," and "reconnecting with the source of our food" was layered over the images. The production value of the film was quite high, and Ellie found herself swayed by the beauty and care presented to her. If anything, she began to understand the draw that the ARC held for Mara, a kind-hearted soul who always wanted to do good in the world.

At the end of that clip, Mara brought the lights back up and the woman on stage said, "Exciting, isn't it?" The eyes of the youth in the audience sparkled and their heads nodded. "Oh, yes – worms and dirt and hard work can be beautifully exciting."

Hazel snickered. The woman and audience looked in her

direction. Hazel shifted in her seat and looked down.

Mara finally noticed Ellie and gave a quizzical look. *Why are you here?* her face seemed to say, but with an undertone of being happy to see her, nonetheless. Ellie smiled. The woman pursed her lips and continued talking.

"For those of you who said that organization was the most interesting thing – you are my people, you organizers – working with us at the co-op would be a fabulous opportunity to put your talents to use."

The lights dimmed and the next clip began. Mara's face was on the screen, hard at work in the back of the co-op store. Ellie felt very proud to see her up there, so smart and so beautiful. Then there were shots of lots of clipboards and computers and carts and spreadsheets being shown. Shots of community members doing their grocery shopping. The voiceover – male this time – talked about "seeing first-hand the difference being made in your community" and "being the one who makes sure each community member receives their fair share of goods." Footage of people sweeping and cleaning, footage of the signs in the store filled with community-affirming mottos and slogans.

The lights came up again. The woman was taking a big breath, smiling. "I just love that. If you love working with numbers and data and like keeping things tidy, I would love to see you on our team with Mara and I." She motioned sideways to Mara, who waved. "I would say we have a special team in place, wouldn't you, Mara?"

Mara nodded. "Most definitely, we do."

It may have been Ellie's imagination, but it appeared as though they stared at each other for just a second too long. Ellie could see Mara squeezing her left thumb with the thumb and index finger of her right hand. That was her nervous tic. A dead giveaway for Ellie if Mara was ever lying.

"And for you "people" people" – a small cheer arose from the extroverts in the audience as the woman playfully did a shooing motion with her hands – "we have, at last, the community engagement team."

Once again, the lights dimmed, and a new short film began to play. There were shots from around the town that earned small hollers from the people connected to them – the library, the gas station around the corner, footage of homes and groups of kids playing in the street. It showed clean cut young people knocking on doors, shaking hands, handing out pamphlets, giving speeches at community events, answering questions.

This time the voiceover consisted of the voices of the team themselves, young people talking about being "the ones on the ground" teaching the community about "our mission and vision" and finding the next "generation of changemakers" to bring into the fold.

As the film was coming to a close, there was a sudden shift in the imagery that seemed to be spliced in and recorded over the original footage. There was some static and then a mostly dark screen with a very dim lamp in the background of a small room. The top of a person's head could be seen in the lower left corner of the screen, close to the camera. It was hard to make out their features, especially with such grainy video. The audience could hear the woman on stage cursing under her breath, frantically pushing buttons and calling Mara for help. The person in the video began to speak.

"It's a lie. The whole thing is a cover. Don't listen to them. They want to" –

The woman couldn't figure out the right combinations of buttons to push and instead resorted to slamming the connected laptop shut. Mara brought up the lights, and for a minute there was a hushed whisper that fell over the audience. The woman stomped over towards Mara who was holding out her hands and shaking her head.

Hazel turned around to look at Ellie. "What. The. Sassafras."

"I know, right?" Ellie said, while trying to catch a glimpse of Charlie and his reaction. He was sitting quietly while his neighbors to the right were chattering away, and Ellie started questioning why in the world he had chosen to be on the community engagement team. He didn't seem to be particularly outgoing.

"Who was that in the video?" Hazel asked David under her breath.

"I don't know," said David. "I couldn't even tell if it was a boy or a girl."

"Me either." Hazel tapped Ellie on the leg. "Do you know who that was?"

Ellie shook her head, breaking her gaze from Charlie's direction. The woman on stage had returned to the center and held up her hands.

"I know, I know that was upsetting. Everybody, please, bring the noise down."

The audience shifted around and looked to her for some kind of explanation.

"I hadn't wanted to talk about recent events in this meeting, as I don't believe in giving any extra attention to people who don't deserve it. But, this video, and other rumors I am sure are going around, show me that there are some things that need to be cleared up before we can go forward, and I thank you for your patience in this." She took a long look around the room. "I am sure you are all aware of what happened a couple days ago? The fires?"

Some of the audience nodded.

"Well…we are still unsure of the exact motivations for that, but what I will say is this – some people are frightened by change. They see change, a new way of doing things, as the enemy. When they feel their way of doing things being threatened, they fight back, sometimes violently." She grimaced. "Here, though, that is not what we are about. We are not about violence here. We are about building a better, stronger world for everyone. The people. The animals. The planet. Obviously, as we can see from the science and the data, which you will get to know intimately if you work with us, the way we have been doing things is working."

She took a few steps, silently clapping her fingers together as she thought.

"Sometimes, to effect change, even a very small one, one must make drastic changes in the way things are done. And change, like I said, can be frightening. It is now our duty here at ARC to keep pressing forward in our mission, to show those who *are* afraid that – " she pointed her finger up into the air, " – we are *not*. We are not afraid to change our future for the better. And you all can be a part of that."

Mara tiptoed across the stage and whispered something in the woman's ear.

"Yes. Good. All right, then – the best way to give you a true idea of your potential with ARC is for you to see it firsthand. We have arranged for some tours to be given throughout the facilities. We have a fairly large group today, so we will need to split you up. You will see on this table down to the right of the stage there are three clipboards, one each for Production – working with hands people; Inventory – organizing people; and Community – *people* people. Sign your name under your appropriate group – or if you are here at the invitation of one of your friends who has already signed up, simply write your name and "so-and-so's-guest" on the form. Everyone will get to see each department today, but we will stay within our chosen groups as we rotate around. After you have signed your name, please exit out this way and workers will help you separate out as requested before we get going."

Everyone began to stand and stretch. Hazel shook her hands out in front of her. "Shizzle cakes. Until that freaky video, I was falling asleep." Ellie could see through her casual demeanor that Hazel was still scared from what had happened at the warehouses, and rightly so. Ellie still felt afraid.

David rolled his eyes at her. "We've been here for, like, thirty minutes is all. You're so lazy."

"I'm not lazy, I'm just smart. Smart people don't spend their time listening to boring presentations."

"Well, if listening to a presentation gets you a job, maybe you just put on your big girl pants and do it."

"Whatever, David. I am just here because you needed to bring someone and you don't have any friends."

The look on David's face showed that her words stung. His eyes dropped. "Don't be a jerk."

Hazel laughed. "It's true, though! But don't worry. I am sure you'll find one eventually."

Ellie piped in before she could stop herself. "I'm his friend."

David looked up, appreciative.

Hazel's smile fell from her face. "Well, kind of. Only because you're friends with me."

"No," corrected Ellie, "I am pretty sure I was friends with David first."

This wasn't untrue – she and David had played together alone the first week or so after the Dixons moved in next door, as Hazel had been sick and was staying indoors.

David's eyes twinkled with thanks. Ellie noticed for the first time how dark green his eyes were. He had mammoth eyelashes that would cause any girl to faint with jealousy. It was his goofy grin that distracted from them.

Hazel shook her head at Ellie. "Unbelievable. A mutiny."

"Technically, this isn't a mutiny. For it to be a mutiny, you would need to be the leader in charge. We all know that isn't – "

" – Ew, gross! Stop being a nerd and stuff!" Hazel playfully punched David in the arm. "Okay, fine. You have one friend."

"One is all I need," David said, gently shucking Ellie under the chin in a big brother kind of way. He then put his hands in his pockets and looked toward the clipboards. His ears were red.

"We should probably get down there and sign the papers," Ellie said, shuffling herself out to the aisle and down the steps toward the stage. When she reached the table, she grabbed a pen from the provided containers and bent over to write her name on the Community form. *Ellie Coleman, Charlie...*It was at this moment that Ellie realized she couldn't remember Charlie's last name. As a child she hadn't really bothered to learn last names, and as they had only lived next door for a year or so, it hadn't ever been important for her to know. It had been on the handle of his tackle box. What was it? She tapped the paper with her pen. "This is embarrassing," she muttered.

"What, that you don't know my last name?"

Ellie gasped and stood up into Charlie who had been leaning over her shoulder, almost knocking the both of them down. His strong arms wrapped around her and he steadied them both. "Easy, girl. Easy."

This reference to her being an animal pricked her feisty spirit and she shook him off. "I'm not a horse. Or a dog. Or whatever you meant."

He spread his arms. "I meant…girl. That is it. Human girl."

She finished scribbling *Charlie's guest*, purposefully not asking for his last name, and then started across the base of the stage toward Mara. Charlie followed, but kept his distance. *Harper*, she remembered. *Charlie Harper.*

Mara was answering questions from some particularly eager participants.

"What is the housing like here?" asked one girl, obviously spoiled and probably afraid of vinyl flooring.

"It's fine," said Mara. "It's nothing fancy but it does the job. They are kept really clean, so that is nice."

"You mean *you* keep it really clean, right? Like, you don't have maids?" asked the spoiled girl's friend.

"Well, we do need to keep our spaces tidy, but they do send around a cleaning service once a month to deep clean everything. It keeps everything, you know, up to standard."

Mara caught Ellie's eye.

"This is my sister," she said, easing herself away from the

questioning hoard, "so I am going to visit with her for a bit and you can catch me later if you have any other questions, okay?" She gave a fairly genuine smile, and then hugged Ellie and whispered into her ear, "Dear God, save me. These tours are the worst."

Ellie laughed. It was good to see her sister, to feel her. Mara could sense that something was different, though.

"Ellie, what is it? Is everything okay?"

"Yes," Ellie said, "and no. I don't know. Mom is here."

Mara's eyes started darting around, worried. "*Here,* here?"

"Not here in the room. But, like, here in town. At the farmhouse."

"Oh, wow." Mara stopped her surprise and checked her volume level. "Why? What happened?"

Ellie shook her head and put her palms out. "She woke up? I don't know. She is acting normal now. I don't know what to say."

Mara's face lit up with hope. "Isn't that a good thing? Like, she's talking and everything?"

Ellie sometimes forgot that it had been a long time since Mara had seen their mother. Any information she had about her in the last two years, she had gotten through Ellie. Ellie suddenly felt very responsible for everything, even though that didn't make sense.

"Talking, cooking, laughing – all of it." Ellie paused. "And yeah, it is good. It has been good. But not. Because even though she is acting normal, it's all still the same old, same old. You know, stuff about dad. The bad people. All of that." Ellie looked around. "Probably shouldn't talk about it here."

Mara nodded. "But, wait – why are you here? Are you seriously thinking of joining?"

Ellie remembered Charlie and turned around. He was waiting about twenty feet back. The girls who had been questioning Mara were now chatting it up with him, and he seemed very comfortable laying on the charm. The girls giggled and he smiled, and Ellie could swear she saw him flexing his muscles under his shirt.

Ellie turned back to Mara and shrugged. "I got invited."

"And who would this be?" a voice rang out from Ellie's right. She turned to see the woman from the stage smiling and clasping her hands in front of her skirt and blouse.

Mara hooked her arm through Ellie's. "Oh, Mrs. Farnsworth! This is my little sister, Ellie."

"Ah," said the woman, looking Ellie over. Ellie felt uncomfortable. "And how old?"

"Sixteen" said Mara and Ellie together.

"Almost seventeen," Ellie pointed out. "In July."

Mrs. Farnsworth put her chin up, looking down her nose, chuckling. "Hmmm. Still at the age where being almost older is a sense of pride. Endearing." She tilted her head to the right. "You look so much like your father."

Ellie looked from Mrs. Farnsworth to Mara and back again. "You knew my father?"

"I prefer to say that I still do. Mara and I have talked about him a lot, in fact."

Ellie looked at Mara. "You have?" Mara diverted her gaze.

"We have," said Mrs. Farnsworth. She raised her dark red, arched eyebrows and something clicked in Ellie's brain. One of the photographs! Back at the berm house! She was the woman in the white coat that had been standing next to Hazel's mom in the picture. At least she was fairly certain. Eyebrows like that were few and far between. "Be assured that there is always hope, and that there are many of us who believe we will find out what exactly happened to him." She clicked her tongue. "I wish we knew more."

Mrs. Farnsworth looked over at Mara and took a big, cleansing breath. "Well! Shall we?" She motioned out the exit door behind Mara. Mara nodded, setting her shoulders back into a professional posture. Ellie followed her and was temporarily blinded by the unexpected spring sunlight. The cement courtyard was not an incredibly inviting place, but it was clean. The corners were filled with pots that had Candytuft overflowing their edges, not yet flowering. Baskets of daffodils were in bloom.

Ellie saw Charlie standing off to the side, those girls still hanging on his every word. Ellie looked away. She wondered if he even remembered she was there.

Mrs. Farnsworth clapped her hands together to get everyone's attention and said in a loud, clear voice, "OK everyone! This is where the real fun begins. If you are interested in working on the farm, please stand over there in that corner. Angela will be the helper leading you on your tour."

A perky blonde girl waved her hand. Her teeth were very white, but her smile was crooked, as if half of her face were paralyzed. She seemed nice, though.

"If you are an organizer, come stand close to me and Mara. And if you are a people person, please stand over there next to José."

José was incredibly handsome, and he seemed to know it.

"Look at that kid, will you? Who could say no to that face? That's why he is on the outreach team," Mrs. Farnsworth gushed.

Mara looked at Mrs. Farnsworth out of the corner of her eye, a bit embarrassed by her leader's awkward comments about a boy half her age.

"You will start with your area of interest first. If this area ends up changing after the tour, no worries at all. This is why we do this, to give you a chance to see what would be the best fit for you. Alright then, Angela- go ahead and start out to the farm. José, you handsome devil, on your way. Mara- shall we?"

Without thinking, Ellie started to follow her sister as part of the organizers group until she felt a hand grasp her forearm gently.

"Ellie."

Ellie turned to see Charlie with an unrecognizable expression on his face. Was he upset? Bored? Worried?

"Come on, we need to catch up."

He gestured in the direction of José's group, which had already exited from the courtyard.

Ellie looked back over her shoulder toward her sister who was waving her group members through an exit on the south wall of the courtyard. Mara looked up to see Ellie and Charlie. She smiled and waved and then exited herself. Charlie tugged on Ellie's elbow. "Come on," he said. "Let's go."

José's group was walking along a chain link fence that separated their sidewalk from the massive green houses on the North

East side of the ARC property. Ellie could see through the chain link into the greenhouse where workers were busy laying out flats of seedling trays, watering starts, and labeling the small plants that were starting to grow. This, combined with Mrs. Farnsworth's comments about her father, caused her to begin missing him greatly. A lump rose in her throat which she struggled to hide.

Charlie had jogged up ahead of her and seemed somewhat annoyed at her lack of enthusiasm.

Ellie blinked away the tears that were trying to form in her eyes and shook her head, upset with herself for being upset.

"What is wrong?" asked Charlie once she caught up to him. "You act like you don't even want to be here."

"Maybe I don't," said Ellie. "I actually don't really know why I am here."

Charlie grew silent and stuffed his hands in his pockets. "Let's at least catch up to the group, OK?" He placed his hand on the small of her back then tried to look her in the eye.

Ellie could not meet his gaze for fear of tearing up again. Why was she feeling so emotional? She had so many unidentified feelings swirling around in her and she didn't know how to communicate this to Charlie. His fingers on her back felt like the entire universe pulled into one single touch. She thrilled at it and she chastised herself for it.

"OK," Ellie squeaked out. "I'm sorry. It's fine. Let's catch up."

José was standing at the front of the group. His tall frame was easy to follow as he motioned to his right for them to enter into a nice-looking building made of brick. It was the Community Engagement Center, which was a place where people could come and see a presentation similar to what they had already watched that morning. It was kind of like one of those cool children's museums places that have a pretend shopping center and other community stations to play at. Ellie had seen pictures of it in the brochures that Mara had brought home, but she had never come to visit it.

She imagined that it was probably one of the most exciting things to do in their small town for any kids under the age of ten or so. It was a smart move for ARC to design it this way, as the children in their community would grow up associating them with fun, which would most likely make recruiting them a much easier task once they were of age. The youngest age that could sign up for ARC was fourteen, but that was on an individual basis. Most of the youth who joined were at least sixteen. It was a guaranteed job in a place where there were very few jobs to go around. You got to live away from home. Get an actual classroom education. Ellie could see the draw. She maybe even started to feel it.

José gathered everybody together at the front entrance doors just inside the lobby. He spread his arms wide and smiled. His copper skin glowed in the rare March sunlight that was streaming in through the glass windows and doors. "I am so excited that you all are here today," said José, his expressive and beautiful face full of animation. "If you join the team with me, you will find that you get to do the greatest, most satisfying work in the world." He waved his arms around as if to show what this very satisfying work entailed. The group members all started to take an expansive look around themselves at the Disney-like environment. Ellie half expected him to break out in song and dance.

Her attention was drawn elsewhere when she spotted some wooden vegetables and fruits that were put mistakenly in the wrong bin to the side of the pretend store. She wanted to fix them. That would be very satisfying.

Charlie followed her gaze to the wooden apple sitting atop the wooden broccoli in the bin clearly marked *CORN*. He smiled and shook his head.

"It's anarchy," whispered Ellie. She started to feel better.

The doors to the lobby opened suddenly and a woman rushed into the room. It was Charlie's mother. Her hands were anxiously playing tug of war with a pair of black velvet gloves.

"Charles? Charles?!" she called out, her droopy mouth hanging open between words.

Charlie dropped his head and cursed under his breath. He then raised his hand to get her attention. Her eyes caught hold of him and then fell on Ellie. Her face soured instantly. She was breathing heavily as though she had been running. Charlie made his way over to her, whispering "excuse me" as he tried to navigate between the bodies dividing them. Ellie stayed put but couldn't pull her eyes away from the scene as José resumed his speech and ventured to show the group around the space.

Charlie's mother pulled him into the space between the glass doors for some privacy. Her face started contorting as she spoke what appeared to be stern words. Her bony finger poked toward him a few times. He looked down the entire time she was speaking until she leaned in closer, said something, and then they both turned to look at Ellie. Charlie put his hands out and shook his head, as if to say, "I don't know why she is here." Ellie blushed immediately and turned away, embarrassed at being caught watching them and angry that he lied. Or at least appeared to have.

Charlie's eyes were so blue. Why did they have to be so blue? Why did she have to care what this boy thought of her? Why did she care that those girls had been talking to him? Or did it bother her more that *he* had been talking to *them*? Why couldn't she just let him go talk to his mother, and, instead of feeling a part of herself pulled away, choose to turn and focus on José teaching the group about greeting community members when they come to the center and which brochures tend to be received the best?

José's words were coming out but Ellie wasn't hearing any of them. Her heart was beating in her chest and she felt as though heat was drilling through her shoulder blades from behind. When the group shifted to another spot and she dared to take a peek towards them, she saw the back of Charlie exiting the outer doors and turning toward town.

viii

some of us stay buried in our own minds

for a very long time

the wish to do more

become something more

remaining dormant underneath

the soiled layers of reality

we've so carefully mounded around ourselves

and in this waking sleep we slumber

until an outside force rushes into our life

a diagnosis

a loss

a role to be played

      that we do not want to play

      but we must play

      because suddenly the world is

      much larger than us

      and we are needed

though we doubt we are up to the task

and we resist

all the while the pressure is increasing

pushing on our walls

for there *needs be opposition in all things*

and it causes our minds to unfurl from the fetal
position

and we know that change is inevitable

and possible

and necessary

that the reserves are there

they were there all the time

and that we only needed something to push against

in order

to emerge

CHAPTER 9

When Ellie was nine her father taught her to swim.

It had been an especially hot summer and Ellie was tired of not being able to join the Dixons when they went to swim off the dock at Hagg Lake.

She had tried to learn to swim one time before, and like all things that she wasn't immediately good at, she called it a disaster and swore off ever trying again. The fear that had paralyzed her, along with the lung-squeezing cold of the water, had been enough to teach her all she needed to know about swimming – it was miserable, and it definitely was not fun like the other kids insisted.

Her father had been very patient on that second go-around. Ellie had spent many minutes wringing her hands on the dock, crying, saying she couldn't do it, and generally making it impossible for him to teach her anything at all. After the sun started to go down, he hoisted his pruned body out of the water and put his hands on her shoulders. "When you are ready, let me know." He gathered his towel, slipped on his flip flops, and started toward their truck that was parked down the hill toward the mill.

Ellie knew that the Dixons were going to go swimming the next day. They were even going to bring popsicles and grill hot dogs. Mara would go, and Ellie's parents. Ellie loathed the idea of coming up with yet another reason for why she couldn't go in the water. She usually ended up sitting on the side of the dock in a camping chair, nursing some pretend toe injury while wearing a life jacket, or feigning a stomachache that magically disappeared when food was around. She was sure that Hazel and David had to have figured it out by then, but she was too stubborn and prideful to admit that she didn't know how to swim.

Her father had almost reached the top of the dock when Hazel called out, "Wait!"

She turned back toward the water and squinted into the setting sun. Time seemed to go in slow motion as she hurtled herself down the dock to the edge and leaped. Time went even more slowly in the seconds between launching herself into space and then splashing into the all-encompassing water. The entry into the lake jarred all of her senses at once. The world was muffled and deafeningly loud at the same. Her legs and arms frantically clawed at the water and propelled her upwards for a short, gasping breath that was quickly followed by another dip below the surface.

She sensed rather than saw her father standing over her. She could hear his voice – *Eliyah!* – and feel the air bubbles fizzing around them as he dove in. His arms grabbed her deftly and held her up for air. She took a gulping, grateful breath and then tried to push him away.

"I can do this!" she said.

"Okay," he said, and let go.

Ellie sank quickly and dramatically. Again, her father's arms wrapped her in safety and brought her back up. "That wasn't me," she sputtered. "You threw me in. I didn't have a chance to get started right."

It was this story that came to Ellie's mind as she crouched behind the corner of Sheriff Jack's building, eavesdropping through a window after following Charlie and his mother. This was how she tended to go through life – forcing herself to get in the middle of things and just cope with them already, even if she didn't quite know how.

She had no idea what she was hoping to find when she slipped out the doors at the Community Engagement Center, but as Charlie was the reason she was there in the first place, she saw no further reason to stay through the rest of the tour, and her curiosity became too much to resist.

She had stayed far enough behind him and his mother that they hadn't seen her, but that also meant she could not hear what was being said aside from analyzing non-verbal cues. Charlie remained fairly stoic the entire walk, his hands stuffed in his pockets, head down and shoulders slumped forward. His mother, on the other hand, was repeatedly jabbing a finger into his arm or chest, leaning sideways into him as she spoke. When she waved her arms around, the pair of gloves she was still holding in one hand would flop back and forth as she gestured. They walked straight to the sheriff's office and went inside.

Ellie had spent many days hanging around Sheriff Jack's office when her father was still around. She knew that there was a small patch of earth that was miraculously free of blackberry vines just underneath his office window, at least there had been, and she was relieved to see that this was still the case. Himalayan blackberry will invade anywhere that it can. As she quietly positioned herself, she felt herself guilty of the same action, but not guilty enough to change her mind.

The window was open just a crack. Their voices carried easily through the opening and Ellie quieted her mind, trying to still her breathing and make sense of what she was hearing.

Sheriff Jack's voice was speaking, calm and steady. "We have you on camera." Some shuffling of papers. A chair scooting.

"This can't be true," Charlie's mother protested. "He was

working with ARC all afternoon yesterday."

"I understand that this is upsetting, June, and nobody is going to jail. We're only trying to get more information, that's all. Something happened behind the mill yesterday, and your son was captured on surveillance camera around the time of the alleged crime."

"Can I see the footage, or picture, or whatever?" Charlie's voice said.

More shuffling of papers.

"I'd say that is pretty much your face, is it not?"

There was silence for a few moments. "Yes. It's me."

"*Charles.*" His mother's voice was filled with horror and disappointment. "Maybe you should stop talking now, until...until..." she trailed off.

"But we didn't do anything."

"We?" Ellie could hear Sheriff Jack tapping his pencil on his leg, something he always did as he thought.

"What?" June sputtered, breathy and incensed. "Why did you lie to me? About working? Why were you behind the mill?"

"I went fishing at the dock. I met a friend there. And then we

IN MY HAND A FOREST

walked home. That's it."

"Who?" asked his mother.

Sounds of squeaks as someone shifted in their chair.

"I'm not going to say."

Ellie recognized the squeaks as coming from Sheriff Jack's chair - the wheeled, leather one her mom and dad had given him for his birthday many years ago. She felt she could hear him leaning across his desk. "And now, why is that?"

"Because they don't have to be in the middle of this. We didn't do anything wrong, we were just there. We spilled some stuff from my tackle box, we picked it up, and then we kept walking home. That is it."

"And you know nothing about the events from earlier that day?"

A slight hesitation. "No."

"Now, see – you hesitated. Which means, you probably know a little something. Maybe even more than just a little."

Another pause. "My friend saw something. I didn't see it. She – *they* – said they saw something as they walked to the lake. But I didn't."

"And what did...*they*...see on their way to the lake?" Jack's voice was careful.

"I don't want to speak for them, sir."

"See, now, we are in a bit of a bind then, aren't we? You won't tell me who she – *they* – are, and yet, they know something that will help me solve a crime. Do you see the predicament you're in?" More pencil tapping. "It's called obstruction of justice. And it could cause you a lot of trouble unless you just start talking."

Before Ellie knew what she was doing, she stood up and said "It was me," through the window. The three of them jumped and turned toward her.

"Hell almighty," Sheriff Jack exhaled.

Once again, she had thrown herself into the middle without knowing what to do. "I'm sorry, Jack. Excuse me, I mean Sheriff."

He was wiping his forehead with his hands and it was obvious that he had been sweating, even in the cool March air. His window did face south and caught quite a bit of sun through the day, but it wasn't even noon yet, and the old building's non-existent insulation was sure to have had zero success at retaining warmth overnight. "Damn it, Ellie, you should not do that. Just...just get in here."

Ellie trotted around the building to the front entrance and

squeezed in through the heavy glass doors. The receptionist, an old woman who had always looked that old as long as Ellie could remember, perked up at seeing her now-infrequent visitor. "My goodness, is that Ellie? Do you want a sucker?" Her corpse-like hands reached into her desk.

"No, thank you, Gertie. I'm okay. I think Sheriff Jack wants to see me."

"He's in the middle of an interview."

"God damnit, Gertie, just let the girl come in!" yelled Sheriff through his heavy wooden door.

Gertie smiled like nothing had happened at all. "He's waiting for you, dear. Go right in."

Ellie turned the round iron doorknob and pushed open the door. Charlie and his mother were standing behind their chairs in front of Jack's desk. She was highly agitated. "My son is not affiliated with that family," she said. "Whatever that girl is saying about my son, she's lying."

They all turned to watch her enter. Charlie's mother picked up her gloves from her seat and started to leave. "Charles, say goodbye to Sheriff Jack. We will take this meeting to be conclusive as to his innocence in the matter. If you need anything else, you can talk to my lawyer." Mrs. Harper left the room with Charlie slowly following behind her, making sure to not look Ellie in the eye as she exited, shoving past her in the doorframe.

When Charlie passed Ellie, he met her gaze. "I'm sorry," his mouth said, silently. She nodded. As he exited the door, he let his hand grasp hers briefly and then he let go, his fingers sliding down and interlacing with hers for the shortest of moments. Sheriff Jack observed this. Ellie blushed.

"Why don't you shut that door?" he asked.

She did as instructed and then sat in one of the seats in front of his desk. He sat back in his chair and looked at her.

"Ellie, how long have I known you?"

Ellie shrugged. "Always, I guess."

He laughed. "Always to you, anyway. You haven't always existed, you know."

Ellie took a moment to consider this. How long had her parents known him? From before she was born?

"Have I ever lied to you?"

Being as there was no way for Ellie to know the real answer to this question, she felt compelled to answer a polite, "Not that I'm aware of."

"Hmmffft." He seemed both annoyed and entertained by her presence. He smiled briefly, and then pulled his scruffy, middle-aged face into an expression of seriousness. "Do you believe me when I say that the things you tell me in this room are confidential?"

Ellie's eyes flickered sideways and then back to him. "Yes."

"Because you know I care about you, right?" His tongue traced around his gums inside his closed lips. "I don't like seeing my Ells-Bells getting mixed up in any kind of trouble."

Ellie stared at the leg of his desk that still had yarn tied around it from when she had laid there keeping herself busy while he and her father played card games well into the night many years before.

"Yes."

He nodded. "Good. I'm glad you know that." He tapped his pencil eraser on his desk top a few times. "How much of that conversation did you hear? Through the window?"

"I know that you know we were behind the mill. Yesterday."

"Hmmm. Yes. Question is, what were you doing hanging around there, at that time of day, just before dark? We have a clear picture of Charlie, but not you. But you say you were there?"

"Yes."

"And Charlie says you saw something."

She nodded.

"Ellie, are you aware that someone was killed yesterday?"

She thought of the man that had been dragged to the back door. Her stomach dropped, and she opened her mouth, stammering.

"I…I didn't know he was *killed*."

Sheriff leaned forward in his chair with worry on his face. "Now, how do you know it was a he? I didn't say if it was a man or a woman, or a boy or a girl, for that matter."

Ellie knew she needed to talk, and talk clearly. "I saw something happen. To a man. I didn't know if he was dead after they…well, after they killed him, I guess." Her mouth felt incredibly dry all of a sudden.

"They?"

She nodded again. 'The men in the truck. The ARC truck."

Jack's jaw tightened. "How did you know it was an ARC truck?"

"It said so. The letters. Right on the side." She reached into her jacket pocket. "I took a video on my phone."

Sheriff Jack sat up in his chair, a little alarmed. "You have a video? Of the murder?"

"No, just right after. I was up in the trees. On my way to meet Charlie at the dock. When I saw what was happening, I decided to pull out my phone and record it." Ellie placed her locked phone on the desk in front of them. The screen was covered in fingerprints.

Sheriff considered this. "Why didn't you call me?"

"I was planning on telling you. I told Charlie I would show it to you." Ellie shrugged her shoulders. "I was feeling a little afraid, I guess. I didn't really know what I saw. It was all really quiet. Not like you would think a murder would be. There was no fighting or anything. They just got close to him, and then he fell down. They pulled him over to the back door and sat him there. I figured they had put him to sleep or something." Ellie played with the fraying edges of her jacket cuffs. "When Charlie and I were heading back home, he wasn't sitting there anymore. I guess I thought he must have woken up and gone home."

"Did you see or hear anything else?"

"Well, the men from the truck…they put a bunch of bags of stuff in the mill loading dock warehouse thing. I don't know the right words."

"Stuff?"

"Yeah, I don't know what it was. Just pallets of these big white bags of stuff. And then they pulled the dock door back down and drove away. That's it."

"And everything Charlie knows is whatever you told him."

"Yes."

Sheriff Jack thought for a minute, tracing his fingers along the wood grain of his desk. "How's your mom?" he asked.

"She's good, I guess," Ellie said, surprised at this change of topic.

Sheriff's shoulders jumped up and down as he let out a small chuckle. The smile lines around his eyes and mouth appeared. "Ells, don't do this. You don't have to pretend."

"Pretend what?"

"That everything is okay." He looked at her phone, nodding toward it. "I can make a lot of things go away if you just help me understand."

"But I didn't do anything. I don't need you to make anything go away."

He sighed. "Ellie, I just need to know what is really going on. Your mom...she's..." his eyes got misty. "She's a special woman. She has helped me through some hard times. I just want to return the favor, is all."

Her tongue felt like cotton. "Do you have any water in here?"

Sheriff Jack turned around and reached into a small minifridge he kept behind his desk. He retrieved a bottle of water which he placed on the desk in front of her and she took it gratefully, gulping it down. "You swear to me that you're both okay?"

She nodded, wiping her mouth and replacing the lid on the bottle.

He hesitated before speaking. "Your dad..." he started, then thought better. "His life was something, wasn't it?"

"Is."

"What?"

"It *is* something." Ellie could feel her ears getting red.

Sheriff blinked and nodded "Is. Yes. You're right." He tapped his eraser on the desk again, thinking back. "Plants and seeds and seeds and plants. Day in and day out with him. The history of it, the science of it, the advancements around it, by god it sounds to be the most boring, awful thing...and yet, when you talked with Joe, he made it the most fascinating thing in the world." He looked out the window and then back to Ellie. "He is a genius, Ellie. A real one."

Ellie felt pride at hearing her father spoken of at all, let alone in such praising ways. Just thinking of him caused some tears to begin forming in her eyes. She blinked them back.

"He had knowledge that was unparalleled."

He swung his chair around and grabbed his lunch box from the back table. He turned back to Ellie with a tub of apples that had been quartered. He offered one to her, but she declined. He bit into one and dug an apple seed out from the still-intact core. He put it on a napkin and pointed to it.

"Do you know what I think about every time I see an apple seed?"

Ellie shook her head.

"I think of your dad." He smiled. "We were right here playing cards one day and he asked me about investments. Like, what I thought about them and if I had savings, or whatnot. I said, 'Hell, Joe, what do you think I am, an emperor? I'm just the damn sheriff. I'm just getting by.' And he pointed over to the tub of apples I was eating and he said, 'You're wrong. You're one of the wealthiest men in the world.'"

Sheriff Jack laughed.

"I said, 'What? Joe, I hate to tell you, but last I've seen they aren't accepting apples for payment down at the gas station.' He said, *But that's just it, Jack. What do they charge money for?* I said, 'Gas. A product. A service. Whatever.' And he nodded and said, *and then what do they go and do with that money?* I thought about it and said, 'I don't know. Pay their bills. Take care of their families.' He said, *by buying apples?* I laughed and said, 'What the hell are you saying? I don't get it.' And he took an apple seed and he held it up and he said, *This here will give you a greater return on your investment than any stocks, bonds, or trades you could ever have. And all you have to invest is some dirt, sunshine and water. All of which are free, if you know where to find them.* He pointed out the window and he said, *This seed will grow a tree that can get up to thirty feet tall. That tree will produce an average of two to three hundred apples a year once fruiting, which can be as early as five years. Each apple holds five seed pockets containing one or two seeds each, depending on the variety. So, within five to ten years, under ideal conditions, this one seed will be giving you a return of two thousand five hundred seeds. If you were to plant each one of those seeds, in ten years you would have five million seeds, from that one generation cycle. If you planted every seed you got from every apple every year, the return would be in the trillions.'"*

Jack smiled at the memory.

"Then your dad picked out the remainder of the seeds in the apples we were eating, put them in my hand, and said *Jack, you're holding an endless apple orchard. There's your retirement. Mother Earth will never let you starve. She is so generous. Those seeds are worth way more than their weight in gold."*

Sheriff Jack chuffed. His eyes met Ellie's as he reminisced. "I was a smartass and told him I don't like apples."

Ellie rolled her eyes and folded her arms across her chest. She liked this. Talking about him.

Jack reached across the table and put his hand on Ellie's phone. "I'll have my technology people pull the video and get this back to you, asap. I may end up needing to bring you back in for questioning later as things develop, but don't worry. You're going to be fine, Ells. You're all the family I've got. Just…stay outta trouble and stop meeting boys by the dock. Who the hell told you that you are old enough to do that, anyway?" His look was fatherly and kind. "Now, get outta here and stop hanging around under my window, will ya? Enough to make man jump right out of his skin."

"Okay," Ellie said, watching him pocket her phone. She couldn't resist asking him a question. "Why doesn't she like me, Jack?"

"Who?" he asked, surprised.

"Charlie's mom."

Sheriff Jack thought for a minute. "Ellie, I can honestly say that when it comes to that one, I truly have no idea." He leaned in a little. "Some people are just sour through and through, Ells. Don't give that old batwing a second thought." He clapped his hands. "Go! Get out! Go take care of that magnificent mother of yours. Do…I don't know, girl things. Go!"

Ellie laughed, feeling better. She stood to go, waving as she exited the heavy door.

Sheriff Jack slid her phone into his chest pocket, patted it, and turned back to his computer, picking up the office phone to get back to work. He held up a piece of his quartered apple and took a bite, smiling and chewing as she closed the door behind herself.

ix

cytoplasm and vacuoles

start to overfill

like tiny wombs full

of amniotic fluid

ready to

burst

and all the life

that is held inside

all that that life

is meant to become

starts pressing

    and pressing

        against the seed walls

no longer satisfied with the space

pushing against the known

reaching for the unknown

breaking free

no longer a mime in a box

no

      it has found its voice

CHAPTER 10

Hazel and David were walking by the police station as Ellie walked out the door, sucker from Gertie in hand. A tiny sprinkle rain had commenced. The sidewalk was dotted with water freckles that had started to bleed into one another.

"Hairy handballs, Ellie! What were you doing in there?"

Ellie held out the sucker, offering it to either of them.

"Was that from Gertie?" David asked, snatching it, pulling off the wrapper and sticking it in his mouth in one motion.

Hazel stared off to an awful place in her mind. "That woman makes me think of dried, white play dough. That's all I can say." She shook her head, snapped back to reality, and hooked her arm through Ellie's. "But, for reals – what's going on?"

"Just talking to Sheriff Jack," Ellie shrugged, taking the wrapper from David and putting it in her pocket. She held out her palm to catch the misty droplets coming down. She tried hard to appear normal, to not give on that she had just learned that she had witnessed a murder the day before. "Checking in."

David's eyes searched hers. She could tell he didn't believe her. She looked away.

"Well, I need time to not be talking about dirt and community values and burning warehouses. I need to eat some junk and talk about boys." Hazel pulled Ellie in the direction of the Dixon home.

"Oh, yeah? What boys?" asked David, smiling his goofy smile around the protruding sucker stick.

The girls trotted up ahead of him.

"Boys who are not *you*," Hazel said over her shoulder.

"Maybe someday you'll broaden your horizons and talk about things that actually matter," David said. "I thought today was interesting."

"You would." Hazel snickered.

Ellie was bothered by the way Hazel dismissed her brother so cruelly and easily. David had always been kind to Ellie, and she had an instinctive urge to stand up for him. "I thought it was interesting, too," she said.

Hazel looked at Ellie. "No way."

Ellie felt defiant. "Yes way. I did."

Hazel stopped walked and looked back and forth between her brother and obviously crazy friend. "Are you guys dork buddies, or something?"

"Dork buddies forever," said Ellie.

David blushed. He turned his head to hide his pink cheeks and started to walk past them, tripping over a root that had grown through the sidewalk. Ellie reached out to steady him. He grasped on to her, and then laughed at his own clumsiness. "Yay for dorks!" he yelled as he regained control of his limbs. He seemed hesitant to let go of her.

Aware of a possible misunderstanding between them, Ellie pulled away, putting her hands up. "Dorks are cool, okay Hazel? Geez. But…what was up with that weird and creepy part of the video? At the end? What is going on at ARC that someone would feel like they needed to…*warn* people?"

David and Hazel grew silent, kicking at random rocks as they resumed walking.

"I don't know," Hazel lied.

The Dixon home was completely in order, as usual. It never ceased to amaze Ellie every time she visited. Ellie was used to not necessarily disorganization, but random resourcefulness. Function over form. Not taking time to consider a decorating color palette or finding the right painting for the living room. Did they have a couch? Fine. Does the stove work? Good. That was as much as either of Ellie's parents truly cared about home design. Her mother cared about having a functional kitchen, to be sure, but agonizing over what finish the cabinets should have was not a part of her considerations. To be in a home where even the little details were attended to and every season or holiday was fully represented in the foyer and main living spaces was otherworldly for Ellie. Even the Kitchen-Aid stand mixer was a custom coordinating color. She loved it and she felt uneasy in it. She loved the beauty of it, the pure perfection always on display. She did not like feeling as though she might mess it up at any moment. Her shoes might mar the light carpet. *Who has light carpet in Oregon?* Should she dry her hands using this towel or the other one? Was it okay to sit in that chair, or was this one just for special guests?

Hazel's mother, Lydia, was in the kitchen making early preparations for their dinner. She startled a little as they walked in.

"Oh, Hazel." She put her hand up to her chest. "And *Ellie?*" A motherly, tender look came across her perfectly made up face. She opened her arms and came to wrap Ellie in a hug. "How long has it been since I've seen my Ellie-girl?" She held Ellie's face between her hands. "My goodness, you are a beautiful girl. So grown up."

Ellie, smiled, a bit uncomfortable with the sudden affection, even though this was someone who she had grown up being around. It had been a very long time since she had seen her. It was an awkward, but not unwelcome reunion.

Lydia turned to wash her hands in the sink before she set to slicing vegetables. "So, how are things?" she asked. Then, after a pause, "How's your mother doing?"

"She's fine!" Hazel piped up. "I saw her yesterday. She is all good." Hazel gave a cheesy grin and two thumbs up.

Lydia looked surprised but also relieved to hear the news. Her flowing blonde hair shook as she spoke. "Oh, you did? Oh, how nice! I am so glad to hear it." She gave Ellie a small, concerned smile. "I miss her, you know."

It was true that her mother and Lydia had been close neighbor friends, swapping cups of flour and watching each other's children, while also discussing world affairs and coming up with business ideas.

"Your mother is very smart," Lydia had told Ellie once. "She should get involved with ARC."

"She misses you, too," Ellie lied. She had no idea if her

mother ever even thought of Lydia. Or even liked her, for that matter. But it seemed the right thing to say.

"Mom, we're going to hang out in my room upstairs. Permission to bring snacks?"

"Sure," she said, slicing an onion and trying not to cry from the fumes. "Just make sure you bring any garbage back downstairs, and roll up open bags and use the bag clips –"

" – I know, Mom. I know." Hazel shot Ellie an exasperated look. "Where's dad, anyway?"

"Hmm?" Lydia inquired, then realizing what Hazel had asked. "Oh, Dad. He just had some unexpected business to attend to. He'll be home soon."

Once the girls grabbed snacks and ran in their socked feet up the stairs to Hazel's room Ellie felt much more at ease. The perfection requirements were more relaxed on the second floor, as company was rarely expected in the bedrooms. Hazel's room was still beautifully decorated in soft hues of ballerina pink, aqua, and sage green set against white everything – white comforter, white furniture, white rug. The walls were the slightest whisper of pink, which was only detectable where the paint met the bright white trim as to give the eyes some contrast between the two tints. Hazel had always said she wished she could have a black room, with black chalkboard paint walls that she could draw on. Her parents were not keen on the idea.

"I don't know why I said I wanted to talk about boys," said Hazel, flopping down on her bed and prying open a bag of pretzels. "There are no new boys in this terrible little town to talk about." She crunched on a few pretzels. "Except for...Charlie." She looked at Ellie with a sly grin.

"What? Charlie?" Ellie waved her away. "He's, like, an old neighbor friend."

"An old neighbor friend who is *back* and *freaking hot*." Ellie kicked her feet around in the air. "You saw how all the girls were falling all over themselves today. That dark hair and blue eyes, man. Unreal."

Ellie had seen. She didn't like to remember it. Charlie had seemed to like it a little too much...but who was Ellie to say what he could and couldn't like? She knew she was nothing to him. Yet, she felt tied to him. She wanted to claim him. She felt jealous just thinking of another girl talking to him. "Hmm," Ellie said. "I wasn't really paying attention."

Hazel rolled over onto her back and made a noise of disbelief. "What*ever*, Ellie. I know you like him. Just say it. You like him." She rolled back onto her stomach, crunching another pretzel. "*I* like him," Hazel said, then, "well, I like looking at him. Staring at his face is the emotional equivalent of going to the spa."

She sighed. Ellie had never been to a spa before. Hazel hadn't either. "I have no idea what his personality is like. But in this middle-of-nowhere place, we've gotta take what we can get. Even if he is a jerk."

"He's not a jerk!" Ellie said, a little too defensively.

Hazel perked up. "Ohhhhhhh. Hit a nerve there, did I?"

Ellie rolled her eyes and sipped on a juice box. "He's not mean, okay?"

Hazel crawled closer to the end of her bed, reaching out to touch Ellie's arm that was draped over the edge of her papasan chair. "How do you know that? Spending much time with him lately?" Hazel raised an eyebrow. "I demand details. Now."

Hazel's pressure to talk made Ellie feel stubborn. "No," she said. Her voice was quivering. Why was she emotional?

Hazel continued to push. "Ellie? Did he do something to you?" She drew close to her friend, her brows knit together. "Because I will kick his finger-licking face in."

"No!" Ellie yelled, and before she knew it, large hot tears were threatening to spill out of her eyes.

Hazel's face showed panic, not knowing how to handle this drastic turn in their conversation. "Oh, friend! What? Why…what is happening?!"

Ellie looked up at the ceiling as the tears came, uninhibited. Her breath came in jagged gulps as she talked. "I don't know Hazel. I just don't even know. I saw someone get killed yesterday, apparently – "

" – What?...What?!– "

" – And I don't know what is happening with my dad, is he dead? And what is wrong with my mom? I mean, she's acting normal now, but, but before….she….I just don't know!"

Hazel crawled into the papasan chair next to Ellie and held her hand, letting her talk.

"I am so sick of this life. Sick of pretending…I don't know…why I am doing it. My parents asked me to do it, so I do it, but…I…don't know why." Ellie's sobs interspersed her speech with shuddering frequency.

Hazel was lost, but not about to interrupt her. She stroked her hand and continued to listen.

"Something…something is not right. With my dad. With what happened to my dad. He isn't dead, he can't be dead…but he might be *dead.* And I don't think it was an accident. But nobody will tell me anything. They all think I am stupid. They're all trying to protect me, but I don't need protecting!" Ellie's voice grew louder with every word. She collapsed further into herself and cried. "I just want to know what is going on. Where is he?" Ellie thought about Charlie, surrounded by those giggling girls. "Charlie can go do whatever he wants. Leave me behind. I don't care." At this statement she cried harder and turned toward Hazel. She had never cried like this in front of a friend. She had never cried like this in front of anyone, that she could remember. It felt freeing and dangerous and necessary and long overdue.

Hazel held her friend quietly for a long while, until the heaving sobs slowed and her breathing grew closer to normal. When she dared to, she tapped the back of Ellie's hand. "How can I help you?" she asked.

The tears returned. "I don't know," Ellie forced out in a whisper.

Hazel shifted to better be able to look Ellie in the face. "Help me understand." Her face was full of compassion and worry. "You said you were sick of pretending. What are you pretending?"

Ellie stared blankly out into the room, unresponsive.

"Is this about your house?"

Ellie turned toward her friend. "You know?"

"Well...no. And yes. Something has been off. For a long while."

Ellie stayed quiet.

"Like…I have learned that I only get texts from you on Tuesdays and Wednesdays. The other days you're, just, gone?" Hazel bit her lip. "On other days I sometimes go by your house to see you." She bent over to look Ellie in the eyes.

"But I'm not there," said Ellie, flatly.

Hazel nodded. "Yeah. That's why I wondered…about your mom…I'm so sorry about that."

Ellie felt something inside of her break at the absurdity of her life. A laugh bubbled up inside of her as she remembered Hazel's erroneous but sincere accusation. It was a troublesome laugh that tugged at the corners of her sanity. She fought to keep it back and couldn't. Hazel stared at her friend who was literally cracking up before her eyes.

"You…thought…I…was a murderer," Ellie wheezed in between cackles.

Hazel wasn't sure whether to laugh along or run for help. "Ellie, stop it. You're scaring me."

"I'm scaring you?" Ellie laughed. "Me?" She almost fell out of the chair she was laughing so hard.

"Ellie!" said Hazel. She looked around in desperation and

then slapped Ellie across the face.

Ellie bolted upright and out of the chair holding her face with both hands. The friends remained still for a few moments, stunned by what had just happened.

"I'm sorry," Ellie said.

"No, *I'm* sorry," said Hazel. "I didn't know what to do."

Ellie slumped back over to the chair and sat back down. Hazel came to put her arms around her friend. "Whatever it is, whatever you need, we can figure it out together, okay? The boys of the world can suck it." Hazel touched her forehead to Ellie's. "But right now, you need to majorly rewind and start over because...you saw someone get killed yesterday? Jumping swizzle nuts! What are you even talking about?"

X

the newborn roots waste no time

snaking out like thirsty serpents

a fractured surge

of growth

seeking water

seeking nitrogen

seeking strength and stability

seeking to go down

in order to lift itself up

above the fertile soil

but first

      a toast

      let us drink to beginnings

      let us drink to the past

      let us drink to all that led us here

      let us drink to what is to come

and the legacy of all those seeds

all the plants that had come before

will manifest in one

like distant ancestors

immigrants

hungry for new shores

determined

to

build

again

CHAPTER 11

Ellie looked out of Hazel's window at the descending afternoon sun. "I need to get back to mom."

Hazel, bleary-eyed from their hours of rehashing the events of the last couple of years, raised herself up from the throne of pillows on her bed. "David can drive you. I'll make him."

The drive back was quiet. Ellie wasn't sure what this new world would entail – a world where friends knew some of their family secrets. Her head started to hurt as she considered the repercussions of opening her mouth like that. She wondered for a moment if she could trust Hazel, but one look at the resolute brown eyes of her friend told her she had an ally, and one she would need. Hazel smiled from the back seat.

David, who had not been part of the conversations in Hazel's room, but could tell, nevertheless, that Ellie was incredibly upset, had insisted that Ellie sit in the front passenger seat and had even opened the door for her like a gentleman. When Ellie shifted to undo her seatbelt once they arrived at the farmhouse, he placed his hand on her arm. "I'll come around," he said. His hands felt warm and large around hers as he helped her up out of the car. For once Hazel didn't tease or comment on anything her brother said or did, which was a sure sign of her exhaustion. David appeared to enjoy this silence immensely. Ellie did, too.

"I'll check on you tomorrow," Hazel said through the rolled down window. The rain was getting inside the car.

Ellie nodded as Hazel hurriedly rolled the window back up. David waited by the car and watched Ellie walk up to the front porch. When she turned to wave he was already getting back into the driver's seat, a burst of rain sending him off. He flashed his headlights to say goodbye and Ellie stepped inside, taking stock of her wet jacket and boots and setting them to dry near the door.

It was dark and cold in the house. Normally a fire would have been burning all day but it was obvious that that had not occurred. Ellie wondered if her mother wasn't feeling well. "Mom?" she called out.

No answer.

Ellie walked into the kitchen. Dark. It was close to dinner time and Ellie's stomach rumbled. She made her way up the back stairs to the bedrooms. One by one she peeked her head inside, only to find them empty and cold. "Mom?" she called again. She had left her, happy and smiling, in the morning before the recruitment meeting. *Have a good time,* she had said.

Of course, Ellie had not told her she would be going to an ARC recruitment meeting, but instead told the small lie that she would be spending the day with the Dixons to make things seem more normal now that they had decided to stay in town for a little while.

"An excellent idea," her mother had said.

"What will you do?" Ellie had asked, a bit worried about leaving her.

Her mother had reached up from the breakfast table and slid her hand up and down Ellie's arm. "Don't worry about me." She smiled, a twinkle in her eye. "Maybe I'll go fairy hunting."

Ellie relaxed. "Not without me, you won't." She had felt a sudden, intense affection for her mother. "Promise?"

Her mother's glorious cheekbones were glowing as she smiled in the cold morning sun coming through the back porch windows into the house. "I promise." She nodded toward the clock. "Now go. Hazel will be wondering who you have murdered now."

"Mom!" Ellie laughed. "That's not funny." It made Ellie think about what she had seen behind the mill. She shook it off. "I don't know when I will be back, but before dinner at least," she had said, pulling on her boots and grabbing her coat with the hood. She hadn't needed to check herself in the hall mirror, since she had already spent an extra half hour preening herself for Charlie, but she stopped to look anyway. The crystalline blue-green eyes of her father stared back at her. Ellie blinked.

"Go!" her mother laughed, shooing her out the front door.

The day had contained so much emotion for Ellie that she truly looked forward to coming home and allowing the warmth of her mother to help soak up the excess. Returning to a dark, empty house was not what she had expected or hoped for, and the stark reality of it made her realize just how much she loved her mother. She had taken her presence the last week for granted. It had been so strange to get used to her being present again that Ellie's walls had been understandably high. She felt she had just been starting to trust her, to trust that she was better, that she was back in Ellie and Mara's life for good.

But now, standing there in the quiet, lifeless kitchen, all Ellie could think of was that plate of lasagna that had stayed in the fridge of the berm house for much too long, and something in her snapped.

"No," Ellie said out loud to herself and to nobody. "You're not doing this, Mom. Not again. You are not leaving me again." Ellie started rushing around the house opening doors as her voice continued to get louder and louder. She stomped up the stairs and through the bedrooms. "You don't get to do this. You don't get to disappear, not again, Mom. Don't do this! You just…No!"

Her face was hot and she found herself surprised at the amount of tears her body could produce in a single day, having thought she had exhausted them all at Hazel's house. The skin around her nose and lips stung when the saline hit it. Her hands pulled at her face, her frizzy hair, her clothing.

"Where are you, Mom?! Mom!"

She felt herself crumpling. She lumbered over to her bed and fell upon it with her full weight, screaming in frustration. "This is not happening!" When her hand slammed into her pillow, she heard a sound like crinkling paper. She sat up and pushed around the sheets and pillowcase until her hands came upon a note that had been stashed out of sight.

Ellie, it read. *I am sure you are scared but don't worry, I am fine. I need you to be brave. I think they found out about the house. I have to go back and put dad's things back where they were hidden. It will be okay, but I have to get there before they do. I left the porch light on for you, don't forget to turn it off before bed. I love you. I'll be home soon. Xo, Mom. PS. Probably best to burn this note.*

Ellie's eyes went in and out of focus and she read her mother's words over and over again. They – who are *they?* She kept trying to repeat *she's okay, I'm okay,* in her mind, but she could not quell the growing sense of alarm in her stomach. She looked out the window. The sun was almost down. The idea of staying at home overnight without her mother felt dangerous and unwelcome even though she had done it many times before. She knew she would not be able to sleep. She had to help. She had to make sure her mom was okay.

She talked out loud to herself as she gathered some supplies in the pocket of her coat for the probably couple of hours' walk in the dark. "It's going to be fine. If they know where the house is, they know. I don't have to worry about that anymore. All that matters now is...I don't know. Just, get there, check on Mom – everything will be fine. It will be *fine.*"

Her fingers were shaking as she went around to lock the windows and make sure everything was secure before she left. As she came to the front door to turn off the porch light and make sure she had fastened the deadbolt, her eyes caught hold of a shadow just outside the front window.

She froze.

She could not tell if the shadow was human or if her mind was just playing tricks on her. Sometimes the way the evening sunlight hit the message tree in the front yard caused strange dances of light to enter the living room...but it was raining. And dark outside. This was a shadow from something under the porch light. Something close.

The shadow moved. Ellie trembled. Suddenly, she was a young girl again.

In her mind, Ellie ran through the fields toward their barn. Her clothes swished. Her heart pounded. She was ten years old.

Her mother and father had always told her this day could come, would come. Her breath caught in her throat and her mind took in the memory of the landscape as if in a dream. The moonlight falling upon the stalks of corn, the tufts of hair at the top of the ears silver and foreign; the barn they built with their own hands drawing steadily closer to them as she hurried along; the oak tree standing bravely off to the side of the south pasture, it's branches and rope swing barely moving, trance-like in the small breeze.

One glance back to their farmhouse had shown the windows dark. *Shut the door*, her mother had said. *Don't leave it open, they'll know if you do.* Was it shut? Had she remembered? Ellie had squinted over her shoulder as she ran, stumbling.

She made it to the barn, but she did not immediately go inside. She went around the back, out of the view of the house and away from the dirt road that led by their land.

Ellie stood on tip-toe to peek in through a hole in the wood. Her eyes danced left and right, assessing. *Okay*. She breathed. *Safe*.

She approached the back entrance of the barn. Ellie saw

where she had scratched her name into the door four years earlier, the summer she had turned six. She thought of how she had smiled as she did it, her deliberate effort to etch herself into history bringing such joy.

The memory cut out as Ellie was drawn back to the present danger looming outside the front door. It was definitely a person. Why they were standing there and what they wanted was an absolutely horrifying mystery to Ellie. Could it be Hazel? Had she forgotten something in David's car? Was it Mom, already back? Jack checking in? Was it…was it one of *them?* As much as she hoped for three of those possibilities to be true, her sixth sense told her she was right to stay still and wait.

The shadow stepped up towards the door, hesitated, then seemed to lean back toward the window. Ellie slowly eased herself closer to the door and back into the corner of the alcove, hopefully out of sight. For all she knew they had been there all night, had seen her wandering the house, screaming as she looked for her mother. She stilled her breath and did her best to remain calm. *Are these the people, Mom? Did they get you? Are they here to get me, too? What do they want, tell me what they want!*

It was now that she saw that the deadbolt was, in fact, not secured. Adrenaline jolted through her as she thought through the repercussions of reaching out to turn it – the noise, the necessary shift towards the window. She was sure to be seen but would have that extra measure of safety in place. Her heart pounded as she thought of all the many ways a person could enter a house other than the front door – for example, the window, right there! Who cared if the door was locked, or even the window itself? One rock smashing through would be the end of that, and any effort she had taken to secure herself inside would have done nothing but give herself away.

Her pulse was so loud in her ears that her stomach seemed to lurch to the beat in her throat. The shadow pressed itself up against the window. Ellie felt as though her heart would explode from its intense, fearful pumping.

She could barely make out the features of a man's face, but it was not an old man. There were no wrinkles, no dark shadows under the eyes, no hunched shoulders. It was a young man. A very handsome young man.

It was Charlie.

Ellie wasn't sure whether to laugh, throw up, scream, or cry. She yanked the door open and hissed in one breath, *"Whatareyoudoingyoufreakyoufreakingnearlykilledmeyoustupidid-iot!"*

Charlie's face looked white and drained. He nearly jumped out of his skin when she opened the door. He fell down to his knees and cursed under his breath. "Good God, Ellie." He put his face in his hands, breathed deeply and then moved forward on all fours to regain his composure and return to standing. It was raining quite hard now, and he was shivering as he stood under the porch awning.

Ellie moved to the side but didn't invite him in. "What do you want?"

His eyes flitted over her shoulder into her cold, dark house. "Are you okay? Why are all the lights off?"

"I'm fine. I'm leaving, so..." she shrugged. "I was turning everything off and locking up."

Charlie gave her a quizzical look. They heard a noise coming from the direction of Charlie's house. His eyes looked again past her shoulder. Without asking, Charlie darted inside and closed the door quickly and as quietly as a mouse. He stood close to her in the alcove, standing still and watching the last of the day's light filtering through the curtains. Ellie breathed in the smell of him. Just a few moments ago she had felt crazy and hurried inside. Now, the energy of his warm, albeit shivering, body calmed her nerves and slowed her mind.

Once certain he had not been seen entering Ellie's house, he turned the deadbolt and swung himself back to face her. "Are you all right?"

She had no desire to go over everything again, after doing so with Sheriff Jack and then Hazel. She had so many words inside of her but also felt empty. She only had energy to stare off into the corner of the room. Everything felt full and fuzzy and heavy and unreal.

Charlie searched her face, trying to force eye contact or get a response. He put his hands on her shoulders. "Ellie? Where is your mom? Are you home alone?" The house was so dark and cold, it was fairly obvious to him that she was, in fact, alone. He ran one hand through his hair. "I've been...I've been worried about you all day. You know, after the...thing at the sheriff's office. I didn't see you come home, and then I thought I saw your mom...Ellie, what is going on?"

Ellie felt like she could finally understand her mother and the desire to go away in her mind. She felt herself start to do so and it felt so nice, so safe. *Go back to when things were right, Ellie, come back to us* her father's voice said.

She felt her worries start to melt and her breathing settle into a full, steady rhythm. She saw the blue sky and she felt a kite string in her hand, and the kite above her was so colorful, and then it was caught in the trees. How would she get it down? She tugged at it in her mind, but her hands didn't follow instructions. Mara was there, and they were young, and father and mother, too. Soon they would nap in the shade and mother would tie daisy chains into Ellie's hair.

Down by the lilies, the willow did weep, her mother sang.

The cairn to be raised and her vigil to keep.

Ellie saw the patterns of the sunlight through the leaves overhead. The grass was soft under her as she lied down.

For under her branches a young maiden lay.

Her mother tickled Ellie's nose with her own.

Never again to don a new day.

Ellie breathed in the blue sky, the sunshine, the grass, the clouds. The air rang with beautiful, full laughter. The world was smiling. It was soft and it was real, more real than anything she had ever felt. She hummed in her heart. She was surrounded by softness. *You are here,* her father said. *You are finally here.* The world folded in around her, tucked her safely away. She felt free and weightless. It was beautiful.

Mara came to lie down next to her. Soon all four of them were side by side, looking up at the clouds and pointing out the shapes they could see. One cloud was especially adaptable. *It's a boot. No, a bunny. No, it's a ship. See the mast, there?*

The ship sailed by and then turned back around towards them. They all held hands as it grew closer and closer, covering them in mist. They were in the clouds now, like a plane, with a blanket of puffy white below. *I'm home,* thought Ellie. *I'm finally home.*

{--------}

Ellie woke with a start. It was dark and obviously the middle of the night.

Where did everyone go? her mind asked.

There was no more grass, no sky, no kites and no clouds. Her hands stroked around herself and felt a bed. Her bed. An arm was draped over her. *Had it all been a dream?* she thought. *Mom is here with me. All of that was a dream. She is safe. No one is coming.*

Ellie turned toward her mother and grasped her hand, breathing it in. Expecting the soft lavender smell of her mother's lotion, Ellie stopped as she smelled the calloused and masculine hand in her own. It smelled of other things, *boyish* things. Ellie shifted back to squint in the weak moonlight as her eyes adjusted.

Charlie laid there beside her, asleep but starting to wake at her movements. She went back in her mind to remember how he got there, how they both had gotten there. *He'll be in so much trouble,* she thought. *His mother will kill him when she finds out where he is.*

Ellie propped herself up on one elbow to look at him, searching her memory for a record of how this scene had come to be. She was careful to not wake him any further. As her eyes grew more accustomed to the dim light his features started coming into view. She studied his handsome face, his hard jawline, his full lips and strong brow arches.

He was so beautiful.

She had no thought that anything improper had happened. She faintly could remember him coming to the house. She had been scared. That is all she could pull from her memory. As she looked at this gorgeous, strong boy next to her, she knew he was there to protect her and watch over her, and she felt a strong urge to snuggle into his body and press her lips at the spot where his jaw met his neck under his ear.

She did not do it, but she wanted to. Every single part of her wanted to. She suddenly felt very grown up and not like a child anymore. She wanted so badly to reach out and touch his face. Instead, she dared to kiss the back of his hand, ever so softly.

Just as her lips pressed to his skin she remembered – Her mother. The note. The...*they*...that were after them. Or after her father, or after what her father knew. She jolted upright in the bed. She had to go. She had to know that her mother was okay. Here she was, lying in her bed next to a boy she barely knew yet loved so fiercely, dreaming about clouds and kissing, while her mother was out there, in the danger, far from Ellie. She got out of bed, waking Charlie. He panicked, looking around in the dark, still blind.

"Ellie? What are you doing? Where are you going? Are you okay?"

Ellie didn't answer, her focus solely on getting herself out the door, flashlight in hand. She felt around for her coat.

Charlie threw back the covers and stood up to shake his limbs, willing himself to wake up and take control of the situation. "Ellie, you are not yourself. Something isn't right. I couldn't leave you last night. You were…strange. Somewhere else. Ellie, stop!"

Ellie tripped into the boots that Charlie must have pulled from her feet and placed at the foot of the bed. She muttered under her breath as she pulled them onto her feet. "I have to go."

"What? Go where? Now? In the middle of the night?" Charlie reached over to the bedside lamp and pulled the cord. The room was bathed in soft light. His hair was disheveled in a devastatingly perfect way. His jeans and flannel shirt were crumpled from sleep. Ellie averted her eyes.

"My mother needs me, and that's all you need to know."

"Where is she?"

"She could be on her way back, for all I know. I just have to make sure she…she's okay."

"Ellie, you're not making any sense!"

"Well, *your* mother is bound to hate me even more now, so maybe you should just go on home." Ellie did not understand herself, why she was being so cold and dismissive of this boy, this handsome, good boy.

Charlie ran his hands through his hair and then took three large strides to stand in front of the doorway. "You're not leaving." He tried to take up as much space as possible. Ellie stood up from getting her boots on and slipped into her coat.

"Move," Ellie said.

Charlie stayed put.

Her voice grew louder. "*Move.*"

"No." He was resolute.

She pursed her lips and pushed at him, gently. "Please. I need to go." She looked straight into his piercing blue eyes, telling him with her soul that it was important. She knew that with her skinny body she could probably slip by if she was quick enough.

He did not move.

Her hands pushed harder against his body and she turned sideways, attempting to escape through the space between his midsection and the door. He shifted his weight and pinned her there. His strength was undeniable. There was no way she was moving this boy out of the doorframe. "Don't make me have to do something awful, Charlie." Her voice was starting to sound desperate. She clenched her fists. "She needs me."

"No, Ellie. I don't know what is happening or where you think you are going, but my instincts say you need to stay in this room. When it's daylight, we can talk about a plan to help your mom."

Ellie gritted her teeth and pushed against him with her full weight. "Charlie! Stop doing this! You aren't in charge of me! I can do what I want! Let me go!"

He braced his arms against the doorframe as she pushed. He didn't speak but simply stayed steady. Her little body trying to move his was like a fly battering at the window. Try as she might, she did not have the physical strength to match his. He didn't lord this over her. She felt an energy of affection coming from him that both calmed her and infuriated her as he refused her attempts to exit the room.

"Charlie! *Charlie…*" her voice was softening. Her fists were losing their power. She began to cry.

Charlie widened his stance and wrapped Ellie up into his strong arms. She melted into him as she felt the full weight of her situation descend once again.

This time it was different, though. When she had talked with Jack, and then Hazel, the weight still fully remained within her chest. This time she felt as though some of it was transferring from her to Charlie, like he was able to take away some of her pain and worry and frustration and fear with just his touch.

She clung to him tightly, never wanting to let go. "Don't leave me," she sobbed. "Don't leave me here."

"Shhhh. Shhhhh," he said as he stroked her hair, placing his lips to her head. "I'm not leaving. And neither are you."

Ellie caught a glimpse of herself in the mirror over her desk. Embarrassed, she pulled back to look him in the face, her tear-stained cheeks red and puffy. "I don't want you to see me like this," she said.

Charlie placed his hands on both sides of Ellie's face, tilting her chin up towards his. His eyes darted back and forth between hers, searching.

"Ellie," he said, "you are the most beautiful girl I have ever seen."

There was no hint of pretense in his words or demeanor. He meant it and Ellie felt it absorb into her every cell.

"Now – we're going to put you back to bed, I'm going to watch over you, and in the morning, we can talk."

Ellie did not want to step away from his arms, but he let her go and stayed his ground in the doorway. He waited as she removed her boots, her coat, and climbed back into her bed. He closed the door behind himself, pulled her wingback chair over from her desk to block it, sat himself in the chair and looked at Ellie, exhausted.

"Morning will come soon," he promised.

They stared blankly forward, each waiting for the other to close their eyes first. After a few minutes, Ellie reached over and pulled the chain to turn out the light.

xi

how does a seed know

which way is

up

when cloaked in earth

on all sides

somehow

    it just knows

    it just feels it

it sends its first shoot upwards

a tiny compass in its soul

with True North

being

    the Sun

the particles of light whisper

their magnetic warmth

drawing the shoot towards them

D.H. RICHARDS

let there be light

come for me

for I give light unto them

that sit in darkness

CHAPTER 12

The morning did not come soon. The night seemed to crawl on and on forever. Ellie thought of her mother and played with the edging of her quilt, rubbing it between her fingers. The air between herself and Charlie was both stagnant and charged with emotion. She kept thinking of the way he had looked at her, what he had said. She wanted so much to believe he really had meant it. She knew he did, but still doubted. *Maybe it was just the moment that caused him to say that*, she thought. *He didn't want me to feel embarrassed or ugly, so he said it.* She worried that maybe in the morning, when the sun came back and revealed her full self again, he might look at her and regret having said that she was beautiful.

Charlie tried hard to sound as though he was sleeping, but she could tell by the way he was breathing that he most definitely was not. They could hear the clock in the hallway ticking away – *Mom must have replaced the batteries this week* – and every sound seemed amplified and intrusive.

After an hour or so, Ellie stopped trying to keep her eyes closed and just let them stare at Charlie. When her eyes adjusted to the light, she could see him looking back at her. Neither of them talked for a while. After some minutes went by, Charlie turned to look out the window. "Why don't you take a picture? It'll last longer," he said, quietly.

Ellie smiled. She rolled over. "Be quiet, I'm sleeping." She could see a smirk on his face through her faintly closed lashes.

Ellie's mind sank back into the memory of that day at the barn. She could hear the way the barn door had squeaked and remembered how her sense of smell awakened, then calmed as it settled into its new surroundings of animals and hay. The sound of something shifting caused her heart to stop. After a few seconds she muttered, *Stupid cow.*

She made her way to the first stall on the left and was greeted with a pile of fresh straw. Ellie wished she could curl up in it and go to sleep right there, no worries of bad people, no worries of anything at all, but she couldn't. Her mother had told her to hide, and the trapdoor to the irrigation cellar was propped open. *I can hide down there.*

Ellie stepped down onto the wooden ladder that led into the dank hole below the stall, grasping the door's thick, metal handle for support. *Can I breathe down here?* she worried.

The soles of her shoes did not handle the ladder rungs very well, slipping out from under her. Still clutching the handle on the center of the trapdoor, Ellie fell to the dark and wet floor below, pulling the heavy iron door closed behind her. The clang of metal against metal reverberated around her in the suffocating darkness.

Her sight was taken. She had fallen maybe five feet or so, enough to hurt but not far enough to have seriously injured her. The standing room in the water splashed as she landed. The water table in Oregon was always so high, especially this time of year, that this room stayed wet most of the time. The smell of mold and moss overwhelmed her. The thick dirt around her had muffled all sounds. It seemed like the few seconds following were frozen in time. Her body kicked in and forced her to breathe. The tears did not come. The fear had been too real.

Each moment passed with anxiety. Cold. Wet. Shivering. No clock to help, no way to gauge time. She had struggled with the desire to yell, wishing she could push up on the door to see where her mother was. She couldn't tell if the strange silence was real or simply the result of the loud bang of the door still ringing in her ears. Every second she was torn between that universal desperation to survive, undetected, and her aching to know what was happening above her.

A sound! Her own fingers scratching nervously on her arm. Another! Her frantic breath. Her mind had played tricks on her, her

221

eyes seeing spots and movement in the pitch blackness. She thought fondly of warmth. Her quilt. Her bed.

One-one thousand, two-one thousand, three-one thousand. She had been grateful for the way her mother had taught her to count through a thunderstorm, to count through her fear. She could gauge how far the lightning was, verbally put distance between her and the danger with a safe barrier of comforting numbers. As she counted it would get farther and farther away. *Four one thousand, five one thousand.* What was she counting for, and at what number would she do something? She didn't know. It calmed her, though, so she continued. *Six-one thousand, seven-*

{----------}

In the morning Ellie was surprised to find that she had, in fact, slept. The clouds and rain blocked much of the sun, making it impossible for her to gauge what time it was. When she sat up, she found her wingback chair put back into place, her door open, and the smell of toast and eggs coming from the kitchen.

It was such a strange sensation to wake up to the knowledge that a boy had been here with her, alone, all night, that that boy had told her she was beautiful, and was now downstairs cooking them breakfast. She felt very much as though they were playing house, and would normally have relished the feeling, but thoughts of her mother came crashing into her heart and mind, taking any joy out of this bizarre time spent with him.

Ellie collected her boots and coat, used the bathroom and brushed her teeth, and came downstairs. Charlie had done his best in a kitchen he didn't know his way around. He had set the table with their mismatched dishes. "Will water be okay?" he asked.

Ellie smiled. "I can't stay." Her stomach grumbled. "I'll take some toast, though." She grabbed a couple of pieces that had already been buttered and started for the back door.

"Hey, wait," said Charlie. "I said we'd talk about a plan in the morning, not that you would just go off into who knows where without me!"

Ellie stopped and turned back to him. He held up her mother's note.

"Does it have something to do with this?"

She snatched it away from him. "Give that back."

"What is she talking about, Ellie? Another house? This house? *They found out about the house.'* Who is 'they'? What do they want?"

"I don't know! Okay? At this point, I don't really care. I just want to know that she is okay."

"Where are you going?"

"I can't tell you."

"Then, I am coming with you."

"No, you're not. I have made this walk countless times. I will be fine, especially now that it's day."

"Ellie, I have to tell the Sheriff. Or my mom. Somebody. Mara. Shouldn't Mara know?"

"I don't have time to worry about any of that right now. Mara is safe."

"Why are you being so secretive? You are driving me insane, Ellie! Just say it! Just tell me what is going on, because I will never stop asking until you do!"

"You're just going to have to trust me, Charlie. Even I don't know what is going on. But I will find out. And this is how I will. But I find out *alone*." Ellie remembered that Hazel was going to check in with her in the morning. She went to grab her phone from the pocket of her coat and found it empty, remembering that Sheriff Jack still had it. "Go tell Hazel that I am okay. That's what you can do. I don't have my phone, so…" she shrugged. "I'll see you when

I see you."

Before he had any time to stop her, she sprinted out the door. She was a fast runner and she made it past the barn in no time. She didn't stop to look back until she was safely past the tree line, and even then, she only afforded herself a moment to turn and see him, a small speck standing forlorn on the back porch out of the rain.

She loved him.

Even though it had only been just over a week since she and her mother had walked from the berm house to the farmhouse, it felt as though the steps she was retracing were an ancient memory. It felt as though she was running down a hallway that was continually growing longer as she went. The faster she pushed herself down the trail the slower time seemed to move. She tripped repeatedly but did not take time to tend to the resulting bumps and scratches, her adrenaline more than making up for any discomfort from minor wounds.

I'm coming, Mom. I'm coming.

The steady, light rain quickly soaked her from head to foot with its thick, misty quality. The tree roots and rotten leaves on the path were slimy and slick. She often had to stop to catch her breath. The humidity in the air was quite suffocating, and she felt she nearly had to drink the oxygen out in order to breathe properly.

As she made her way her mind raced around through time and space. *Charlie. Mom. Mara. Hazel's room.* David's hands pulling her out of his car. Charlie's hands on her face. Her father's face the last time she saw him. Her mother laughing just the day before.

Her mind settled unexpectedly on a memory. They were all gathered around the kitchen table at the berm house, playing a game soon after moving in. Risk, was it? Ellie had been too young to remember exactly what they had been playing, but she knew it was a game that required strategy and patience, both things her mind had neither of at that age. Mara and their mother had carefully sorted out the little pieces and set up the board and tried to explain what the process was to Ellie. Dad broke into the conversation, holding his hands out to the game board. "Where are the seeds?" he had asked.

"Huh?" said Mara, giving him a very preteen look of disbelief. "This is a *war* game, Dad."

"Exactly," he said. "That's the way to win any war." He leaned across the table and wagged his finger at Ellie. "You control the seeds, you control the world."

As she smelled the pine-laden air, she thought of the years spent by his side, collecting seeds from the garden and wondering why he went to such painstaking efforts every season. *There aren't many of us left, Ellie. Not many at all.* He labeled them like children, with such pride. *These tomatoes were spectacular this year.* How could he, this simple but genius man, be controlling the world from this little pocket of Oregon, all on his own?

The answer was simple – he wasn't. He wasn't controlling anything at all but his own world, a world that was untouched by the outside. She suddenly held the berm house with more sacred care in her heart. She could see it now as he saw it, a temple of self-sufficiency and love for the earth. A compendium of miracles. Generous, self-sustaining miracles.

But, maybe...maybe he knew who *was* trying to control the world? Maybe he knew something, knew about things he shouldn't have? This was entirely possible, as he seemed to know so many people and had worked so prominently in a small field of science. Maybe he'd uncovered something, was holding on to something. She thought of the big box that her mother had dragged out of the hidden storage room. She thought of the people, the bad people, and found herself again inside of that cellar in their barn as she walked along.

She had climbed back up the wooden ladder and reached her hands above herself toward the door. When the cool metal met her fingertips, she frantically began pushing up against it. *I have to get out, I have to. I don't care if they hear me or find me, I want to be with my mom.*

The door was very heavy, and her frail strength did little to lift it. She began panicking as she pushed harder and harder on the metal. Each attempt was met with little other than a quiet creak, as if the door were an adult complimenting the small child on her efforts.

She quickly became tired and climbed back down the ladder, again immersing her ankles in the murky, foul-smelling water. After a while, she could no longer stand. She sat herself down, the water not feeling quite as cold as it had before. Her shivering wasn't as nearly as intense, either. She crossed her arms and sat up with her knees against her chest, so that as little as possible of her body touched the ground, beginning to rock as she cried.

All she could remember of what followed next was numbness. Darkness. A length of time that, to a ten-year-old, seemed endless and dooming. Her mind started to play tricks on her. Flashes of light would streak in front of her eyes. She shut her eyes tight against the display, only to find the swirling dots behind her eyelids just as disturbing. As time crawled on, she scarcely noticed herself leaning further and further toward the water, until it felt a very good idea to lie down. *I will just wait here,* she thought.

She let the water surround her completely. It was high enough to cover her ears as she lay on the ground, the same height of her bathwater as a very small child. No matter how much she begged for more water, she was always refused. *It isn't safe,* her parents would say. *This is plenty.*

As she lay waiting, she thought of swimming with her father at the lake, learning how to float. Once she had finally dared to try, his hand had felt so comforting on her back, his voice soothing and encouraging her. *Relax, darlin', relax. Let it hold you up, don't fight against it. The minute you fight, you sink, see? Breathe in slow, sweet girl. Feel that peace. You won't fall, I got you, I got you baby.*

Her eyes felt heavy. She wanted to see the lights again. The cold was gone. She actually felt warm. Her shivering had stopped. She felt peaceful.

See Daddy, I am doing it. I'm not fighting.

She closed her eyes and enjoyed the quiet dance, the funny underwater sounds that soothed her ears. The lights were slower now, less bright. *They feel tired, too. They need a nap like me.*

She watched a swirl of dots as they settled down. Her mind began to do the same, drifting into a dream. After a few minutes, her eyelids suddenly glowed orange, veined with red. Startled, she opened her eyes. She saw light! There was light above her, pouring in like the water, flooding her. Still she lay, confused, closing her eyes against the piercing brightness. *You are too bright, light. You took away my dots.*

Venturing to squint one more time, she saw a face peer into

the room from above, but she couldn't make out any features. She smiled. *They've come for me. I will see my mother. I will get my quilt and I will see my mother. They are not so bad, mother, see? They aren't bad. They are helping me.*

A voice called out. Their words were muffled by the water in her ears. *Can't you see I am swimming here?* she thought. She watched as one foot and then another stepped down onto the rope rungs. She could hardly feel the strong arms that scooped her up from the water because of the numbness. She began to feel afraid as she was slung over a man's shoulder. Inside her mind she fought, kicking and screaming, but her body made no such attempt. As she was laid down on the barn floor, her eyes took in one look at the wall of wood before her mind became as black as the room that had held her prisoner.

It felt as though days had passed before Ellie finally crossed the creek and began mounting the small embankment that connected to the entrance of their meadow. Her breath was ragged, and she felt winded and foggy. Terrible thoughts coursed through her brain, a daymare of scenes where her mother had gotten lost, hadn't been strong enough to make the journey, and now lay helpless somewhere, waiting for Ellie to find her. *Stop, Ellie. Stop. She is fine.*

Ellie's wet clothes clung to her much like they had in her

memory, and she was sure to have chafed thighs from the brutal friction of soaked denim on a long walk, but her mind wasn't caring about those things just then. She was near the berm home, close to her mother, and ready to take the past – all of it – and set things right in their world. *I'm coming, Mom. I'm close.*

Even though her relief at making it back home caused her to want to call out, her survival instinct stole her voice from her. She knew it safest to survey the surroundings, safely hidden, before yelping out her presence. She carefully made it all the way up the embankment, and as she did, all of her memories, all of the rain, her wet clothes, Charlie, the whole lot disappeared into nothingness as she took in the scene in front of her.

It was the smoke she noticed first, hissing and spitting as the rain fell, little trails of it wisping up from the remains of their berm home. The hollowed-out hole in the earth where their home had been tucked was a blackened recess of charred, smoky remains. The hill gaped like a cauterized, open wound. She could barely even tell that it had been her home. True, it had never looked like a regular home to begin with, but now it was entirely unrecognizable. There was no door, no walls, no furniture to speak of, only piles of carbon, a metal shell, and sodden white ash.

The support pillars inside were bent and compromised, hardly able to bear the weight of the enormous mound of earth above it. Clumps of dirt had begun to fall from above, the beginning of the collapse. Before long, the entire front of the hill would cave in on itself, burying any evidence that a family once lived here, gathered around the table here, planned for the future here.

Ellie looked frantically right and left, surveying the property beyond their home for any sign of her mother. "Mom?!" she called out. *"Mom?!"* She was drawn to the burned mess even though she knew there was nothing left there to see. She stopped at the edge of where her home should have been, *would have been,* had she gotten there earlier. *Why did I let Charlie keep me from coming? How stupid could I have been?* She grasped to make sense of what she saw. *Did Mom do this? To protect us? To…hide something?*

If their home had been free-standing in the middle of the field, it would have been unlikely to have burned fully with all of the rain and moisture in the air. Being a berm home, the surrounding earth acted like an oven, containing the heat, shielding it from the rain above and allowing the flames to echo their destruction in every direction. Ellie wondered how long it had burned before the walls had given way. Her heart pounded in her chest. "Mom?! Mom, where are you?!" *Did she already head back for me? Did we miss each other on the trail?* Ellie refused to let her mind consider any darker alternatives.

She stepped onto the burned ground. The acrid smell was overwhelming, and the heat still emanated from the back recesses of earth. She stood where the family room would have been, with her room to the right, and the kitchen and her mother and father's room to the left. Now it was all one cavernous, blackened space. The heat radiated through every pore of her clothing. Her shoes began to melt under her. She skipped across the baking surface like a kid running barefoot across the street in the dog days of summer.

Ellie came to the spot of the former kitchen. Just past it, the entrance to the hidden storage room was closed, the heavy metal door proudly untouched by the flames. Without knowing why, she ran to the door and grabbed the knob, turning it hard to the right. The heat seared the flesh of her palm and she cried out, letting go and grasping at her forearm in response to the pain. The burn across her hand was red and angry. She shook it and ran back out into the rain, falling to her knees and planting her palm firmly in the wet grass. She screamed as the second wave of pain rolled through her. She held it there for as long as she could stand, and then pulled her palm gently inside of her coat sleeve to protect it as it throbbed and swelled.

She stood up clumsily, turning back toward the charred remains. *Mom got here in time. I know she did. She got the things she needed to hide before they got here.*

"It's only me, Mom! Mom, you don't have to hide anymore!" she called out to the trees surrounded her.

There was a sudden crash as the skylight that had been positioned over her parents' bed fell from the soggy, muddy overhang, bringing a large chunk of the overhead earth with it. The surprise caused Ellie to jump and then run back to the storage room door. *I have to know,* she thought. *I have to.* Her adrenaline went into overdrive as she pulled her left hand inside of her coat and used it as a glove to turn the handle. The heat burned through the material quickly, and she fell into the room, gasping at the overwhelming and painful effort that it took. The weighted door swung shut again behind her with a clang.

She could hear herself whimpering as she examined her coat, her delirious mind choosing to focus on the least of her worries. She felt as though she were no longer in her body as she crawled back toward the first turn in the storage room. She felt as though a different energy was moving herself along, something that wasn't her. Something more raw, more powerful, more desperate.

"Mom?" she asked, barely a whisper. "Mom? Are you in here?" Her voice echoed strangely in the hard, serpentine space. After a few deep breaths she gathered the strength to get herself fully into the room and crawling on all fours. Doing so without the use of her right palm was difficult, but she balanced on her knuckles the best she could, her hand throbbing from the pressure on her wound. She started to make her way slowly through the first section and then turned the first corner to the right and continued back. The cement was hot but grew cooler the further she went.

Ellie tried to feel around her for signs of the shelves and bins and packages the room once held and found them all intact. This gave her a triumphal boost as she pushed herself along in complete darkness. She kept her left side against the cement wall as a guide. Her knees were rubbing raw inside her wet jeans, and she could feel that at least one knee had a spot that was worn through. She bit her lip and groaned as she propelled herself forward, not sure what she was looking for, but determined to find it, nonetheless. The air felt more and more depleted, as if the greedy fire had borrowed all of the oxygen and never returned it.

As she made it along the outside wall of the last turn, she began to feel more debris around her, and then stopped abruptly when her shoulder hit the one set of metal shelves in the room, still partially bolted into the cement wall. She used her left hand to feel along the shelves of bags and boxes in front of her as she crawled until her hand fell upon something. It felt like leather. She picked it up and sat back on her haunches, using her left hand to place it in her lap and play detective with only her sense of touch to guide her.

It was a shoe.

When Ellie had been twelve, her mother had asked her father for a nice pair of Italian leather shoes for Christmas. They had just been putting the finishing touches on the berm house, and cash was tight. Ellie had seen the look in her father's eyes when he turned away from her after winking and saying, "I'll put an order in with the elves." His eyes looked sad. There were no elves.

When her mother had opened the package Christmas morning, Ellie had looked at her father with as much surprise as her mother did. The twinkle was back in his eyes. "Joseph," her mother had said. "They're just beautiful." She slipped them on right away, the smooth leather loafer conforming to her foot as if they had been designed just for her. She had worn them all day, "to break them in."

Ellie's fingers traced along the soft heel and supple arch. She gingerly slipped her hand into the shoe, filling the space that had been permanently filled by her mother's foot every day since that very Christmas. She closed her eyes, not against the darkness, but against what she knew she was about to find.

"Mom?" she finally called out, softly. "Mom?"

Ellie put the shoe to the side and crawled a tiny bit further in that direction, afraid to reach out. Her hands shook as she felt around herself. It was another two feet or so until she felt the soft shape of her mother's foot under her fingertips. She patted along her leg, relieved to feel her intact, relieved by her presence, relieved by the chance she had to save her. Forgetting about her burned palm, both hands reached out to race across her body, to read her mother like braille, hold her and shake her awake.

"Mom?"

She was sitting up in the corner, her body curled forward around something in front of her as though she were protecting it.

Ellie's hands grasped hold of her left shoulder and felt upwards to her chest and face. Her parched mouth gaped open, unmoving. Her dry lips crinkled like autumn leaves under Ellie's touch.

Her chest was still.

Very, very still.

Her mother's left arm fell down by her side, and something rattled as it fell with it. Ellie reached out and felt for her mother's hand. Her hand was still grasping something rough. Ellie's fingers lightly traced the object and deduced a burlap bag, one of many they had on the property. She let her hand rest on her mother's, already grown cold. She felt her wedding ring, her slender wrists.

"Mom?" she asked. "Mom." A lump grew in her throat. "Mom, it's going to be okay." Ellie stubbornly nodded her head against her rapidly forming tears. "Mom." She shifted closer. Mom."

She did not hear her own moaning at first. By the time she realized that the sounds around her were coming from her own self, she no longer cared, nor had strength to control them. The cries and moans were all that existed right now, the audible representation of so much sorrow and guilt. The fact that she could not see her mother's face made her cry even harder, until her sobs and the shock caused her body to start shaking. She suddenly felt very cold, very angry, and very confused. She reached out for her mother again and shook her – softly at first, and then harder and harder until she heard herself screaming.

"Mother! MOTHER! Don't do this to me, Mother! No! You don't get to go away, you don't get to leave me! No!" Her screams began to soften into a pleading cry. "We can stop them, Mom, I know we can, Mom, just wake up so we can go, I'll help you find your other shoe, please…please, Mom...Mom....I can't do this without you!"

Ellie collapsed into her mother's unresponsive body, her tears still streaming, her voice hoarse from the smoky air. Her throat burned as she sobbed into her mother's hair, thinking of the fear she must have experienced while trapped behind the flames, unable to escape, breathing in the smoke, knowing she would die. "I'm sorry," Ellie's rough voice whispered into the darkness.

I'm so, so sorry.

Ellie's breathing slowed as her left arm closed in around the remains of her mother. *What if I just stayed here?* Ellie wondered. *Would I ever be found?* She knew she couldn't just leave her mother there like that, *wouldn't* leave her.

There was a seismic shift in the earth. Ellie sat up and listened. There was a big *clomph* sound, as though a big, wet giant had fallen to the earth. The back-and-forth layout of the concrete room caused the sound to be both muted and amplified. A few seconds later, another *clomph*. Ellie's grief-stricken mind pulsed with the reality of what it meant:

The ground was caving in outside the door.

Panicked, Ellie used all of her strength to stand. She tried to shift her mother's body in order to hook her arms underneath her so Ellie could lift her or drag her without tugging on her seared palm.

It could not be done, no matter how hard she tried.

The rush of resulting sadness gave Ellie a sudden boost of adrenaline and she managed to shift her mother and pull her a few feet back towards the end of that section of the room. *Clomph. Clomph.* She tried to pull her a few feet more, but she felt stuck. Ellie pulled harder, apologizing to her mother and she yanked at her lifeless body. *Her dress. Her dress is caught on the shelves.* The ground shook and she heard some metal creak.

She knew she was out of time. If she didn't get out, the ground would swallow her up – swallow them *both* up – and there would be no saving her.

She gave one last sobbing tug at her mother and then dropped to her knees, kissing her forehead through hurried whispers. "I love you Mom, I am so sorry Mom, I am so sorry…"

It felt impossible to tear herself away, but she knew she had no other choice. Not if she was going to find her father. Not if she was going protect Mara. Not if she was going to make sure the world knew what had happened to her dear, sweet mother, on this awful, awful day.

"Who did this?!" Ellie screamed as she began to drag herself back through the serpentine cement walls. Her cries were hysterical and brash. *"I will kill you!"* she yelled out at the unknown foe.

Remembering that her mother had been holding something, clutching something, she turned back just as the ground shook again. She knew she would probably never make it in time, but she had to try. Gathering every bit of strength she had, she hobbled her way back to her mother, reached down to rip the burlap bag away from her already stiff fingers, and then made her way to the entrance of the room, limping and sobbing.

She reached the door and used her coat as she had before to yank it open, using her body as a doorstop to keep it from swinging completely closed. The weight of it smashed her against the already-forming mound of dirt that sought to keep her inside.

"No!" Ellie cried. "No!"

She struggled to free herself by trying to climb while clawing through it, only to receive another deposit of earth upon her head and torso. The weight of it pinned her to the mound that was already blocking the entrance, about three feet high. She wriggled her body, trying to free herself from the dirt and debris. She did not realize that a piece of corrugated metal was slicing into her side as she moved back and forth. She pressed against the door with her feet with all of her might.

Her lungs were again full of dust and smoke and ash. She heaved and coughed as she fought and gained ground. She wriggled and loosened the dirt just enough to break free and crawled the side. She did not have the strength to crawl any further, to move, to *blink*, but she knew she had to get fully out of the way.

One section of the overhead earth still hung on, but just barely. She rolled herself and the burlap bag like a small child rolls down a hill out to the wet, grassy acreage adjacent to where her home had stood. Lying on her side, blades of grass obstructing her view, she watched as the front of the hill fell in upon itself.

Their beautiful hidden home was now hidden forever.

A mangled landslide of mud and metal covered every hint of the scene, sealing her mother in, surrounded by what remained of her father in a beautiful, horrible family grave.

xii

emergence

is such a beautiful word

full of hope

birthing

uncovering

unfolding

surfacing

a coming out

how glorious to behold

    that little peeking of green

    its first foray into the world

    the two seedling leaves taking

    their first real breaths

and through all of our admiration and praise

we cannot see the sadness

an exhaustion earned

through standing upon

the very wombs

that gave it life

a departure

a leaving behind

hoping its abandoning

proves worthy

CHAPTER 13

Ellie didn't remember the trip back to the farmhouse. The hours that followed the awful ordeal at the berm house were a jumbled mess in her mind. She couldn't be sure if she had passed out or not, but her first recollection afterwards was that it was suddenly almost night again, so that seemed most likely.

It wasn't until she entered the empty farmhouse, locked all of the doors, and stripped her ripped, filthy clothes from her body that she fully took in the extent of her injuries. The burn in her palm smarted horribly as she showered herself, trying to do all of the work with her left hand while her right hand stayed out of the curtain and away from the pelting water. The bruises that decorated her legs were angry and blue. She gently cleansed the wound in her side, thankful that the cut hadn't gone any deeper than it had. She had no idea how it got there, nor did she want to know how.

She felt as though she had become a robot without emotion.

She felt empty and strange. As she rinsed the soot from her face and hair she tried not to think about her mother, about leaving her there. *I had to do it. There was no other way.*

She carefully toweled off and pulled the first aid kit from under the bathroom sink. She did her best to dress her wounds with the supplies she had at hand, taping gauze across her side and palm. She dressed herself in the softest, warmest clothing she could find. She removed her mother's soft cashmere sweater from her parents' old wardrobe in the dusty bedroom. The dust in the room seemed so miniscule compared with the day's earlier mess.

As she pulled the sweater over her head, she caught a faint whiff of her mother's perfume. A lump rose in her throat, but still the tears did not come.

She had no way to call the Sheriff, since he still had her phone. It was now very late, and she hadn't the strength to walk to his home located halfway around Hagg Lake. There was nothing to be done but wait until morning, when she would get herself to his office to share the awful news.

Before Ellie climbed into bed, she sat on the edge next to the burlap bag. It still smelled awfully of smoke but she did not care. She untied the top and pulled it open, peering inside.

Unable to determine the contents in the dim lamplight, she decided to dump them out onto her desk. Little gossamer bags came spilling out, each one cinched and topped with a name tag. They were seeds, all of mother's and father's favorite varieties. Her mother's tender cursive and her father's all-capitals scrawl flowed from the tags into Ellie's heart. *Nebraska Wedding. Musquee de Provence. Bee's Friend.* Ellie held each bag in turn with reverence. *Lemon Balm. Waltham Butternut. Calville Blanc de Hiver.* She held their legacy in her fingers, a tangible connection to the people whom she loved most.

There was one gossamer bag that did not hold seeds. Inside, she found a folded paper that was old and yellowed. She carefully opened the creases, one fold at a time. The lines had faded but her father's handwriting was still legible.

He had written a list of names:

William Blackwell

Lydia Dixon

Rhett Dixon

Akshay Acharya

Nola Farnsworth

Dean Vanders

June Harper

Jack Rowland

June Harper? *Charlie's mom.* Sheriff Jack? The Dixons? Ellie thought she remembered Mara introducing the woman on stage at the ARC community meeting as Mrs. Farnsworth, but she couldn't say for sure. The other names she did not recognize in the slightest.

Why had he written these names? What did it mean? She couldn't shake the feeling that it meant something bad. That these people were in on something. Just as her father had been.

For the first time Ellie considered the idea that perhaps her father had not been innocent in this tangled mess. What if he had been guilty of awful things? One thought of his kind eyes and she banished the notion from her mind. *No. My father was a good man. IS a good man.*

Unable to make sense of this new information, Ellie decided to climb into bed, bringing the burlap bag with her. She had carefully replaced all of the items within it and held it in front of her in the same way that her mother had. She formed her body into a 'C'. Her quilt surrounded her wholly, as though she were being cradled by her own creation. Hers and her mothers.

Giving herself permission to melt into the night, the tears finally felt safe enough to come. They came in soft, heaping waves. She wept softly through the night, waking fitfully every hour or so to replay the horrible scene in her mind.

In the morning, her eyes opened slowly. Her eyelids felt like sandpaper and she could acutely feel every bump, bruise and burn she had sustained the day prior. Her head pounded with a throbbing headache, the result of so much crying and grief.

She did not relish what she needed to do.

The walk to the Sheriff's office was slow. She had taken the items from the wooden box in the wall, added them to the burlap bag, and tucked the whole lot inside her mother's jacket to show Mara when she got to the co-op. It was a little hard to distribute the contents evenly to hide the bulky shape, but she managed. Her own coat had gotten ruined in the charred aftermath of the day before, and she had tossed it into the outside garbage can on her way out the door. *One less thing to remind me.*

Her eyes caught hold of something in the message tree. She grew closer and looked down to find an antique key with a folded note underneath it. She put both in her pocket, too emotionally exhausted to read what Charlie had written.

Her mind battled with itself - one part of her brain tried to rehearse ahead of time what she was going to say and how she would say it; the other part simply wandered in and out of reality, not wanting to engage in any kind of concentrated thought for the time being.

It was a dry day, thankfully – or at least it was starting out to be. The rains from the night before still clung to the vegetation and the air was rich with smells of the Oregon earth. The moss appeared especially green, and Ellie ran her hand along the covered rocks that ran along one side of an abandoned neighboring farm. That family had been caught saving their corn the year before. They claimed to have been keeping it to grind for cornmeal, but the courts didn't buy it. *How can we be sure? Best to be safe.*

The spongy moss brushed at her deliberately passing fingertips. She did not do this to elicit any joy from the sensation, but rather to use some kind of sensory input as a reminder of her existence, a replacement for pinching herself or slapping her own cheek. She could feel herself wanting to question everything she had experienced the day before. It didn't seem real. It seemed very far away. Time had crawled by. Had it truly happened?

In the depths of her heart she knew that it had, and that now she had to tell Jack, tell Mara, and then...

She didn't know what came next.

What would happen to her now? She was only sixteen, and Mara lived at ARC. It was possible that they would let Mara come home given the circumstances, but did Ellie want that? To hold her sister back? *No. I won't do it.* She would truly prefer to be on her own, which she knew Jack would not allow to continue. But where else could she go? And did she want to?

The years of caring for her mother and walking back and forth between homes had built an independent resiliency inside of her that would be impossible to abandon entirely. She found she did not fear the idea of being alone at the farmhouse, though she would much rather be there with her parents and Mara and somehow erase this terrible and confusing history from their existence. If she had to choose, she felt those were the only options she could accept: either all of her family would be there, or she would live there alone.

*And now that Mom...*Ellie thought, then stopped herself before she descended into the sadness that tugged at her every breath. *There's no 'all of us' anymore.*

She imagined that Jack would probably try to convince her to stay with the Dixons, who would most likely be happy to take her in, but the prospect of conforming to the perfectness required in that environment made Ellie's insides squirm.

She would simply have to stand her ground. He might be the sheriff, but he would have to understand.

When Ellie entered the office, Gertie wasn't at her desk to greet her with an offer of a lollipop or butterscotch candy. Ellie could hear Jack's voice coming through the slightly propped open door of his office. A sign on Gertie's desk read "Off to See Grandkids." A small bowl of dusty ribbon candy sat next to it.

Not wanting to interrupt him, Ellie sat on the wooden bench against the outer wall of his office and waited for him to wrap up whatever he was doing. It sounded as though he was on the phone.

"No, no, I believe it was done rather quickly. Rhett's drone led them right there. They were pretty thorough, I have to admit. I thought for certain we'd find more on him, but I don't know. He's good. We've always known that."

Silence as he listened to the other end.

"Yeah, now it's just how to approach it, you know? I mean, you saw her run off. She had to have gone there, I mean – where else would she go? I made doubly sure that they had extinguished everything before they left. She wouldn't have been in any danger."

Ellie's insides started to burn with awareness at what she was overhearing. Was Jack talking about her?

"And you saw them come home last night?" Pause. "Well, saw a light on in the house, you said?" Pause. "Mmm, hmm. Yes, I will go check on them. Gertie's not in today, so I'm kind of holding down the fort. I'll head over in the next hour or so. I've still got her phone, so she doesn't have a way to call me anyway. I'm sure they're shook up."

Silence.

"I'll write up the report as they give it to me. No official records until then." Pause. "All right. We're getting closer." Pause. "Yep. Thanks for your help, Charlie."

At the sound of his name, Ellie's stomach dropped to her feet.

Charlie?!

All of the anger, all of the grief, all of the fear and pain she had ever experienced in her life combined all together at once inside of her, filling her with a most seething rage. She felt herself float with hatred to Jack's door. She yanked it open and stood in the doorway, her face a full accounting of what she had been through in the previous 24 hours.

"You," she said. For a couple of seconds, it was all she could get out.

Jack looked up from his desk, startled. His wide eyes took Ellie in, and you could tell by his facial expressions and stupor that he was trying to race back in his mind to account for his words and what she may have overheard.

"You. Did. This." Her teeth were bared by her retracted, tense lips.

"Ellie! Ellie. What's going on?" he stood up from his desk and came around with his arms open. She pushed him away with a force he had never felt from her slight frame.

"You know exactly what's going on, Jack." She stepped away from him, around to the other side of his desk. "You. Know. *Exactly.*" Ellie's anger started to take on a form that frightened even herself. She found that she no longer had any deference whatsoever to social custom and norms, what was acceptable or not acceptable to do. All that mattered was the white-hot, terrible ferociousness in her veins that sought to harm anyone and anything in her way.

She grabbed hold of the trinkets on his desk and flung them to the side, smashing his coffee mug and spraying the still hot beverage in every direction.

Jack covered his face and shrank back from her fury. "Ellie! Stop this! What the hell's goin' on?"

Ellie started pulling open drawers and throwing files around the room, papers snowing down from the ceiling as she tossed them with contempt.

"Ellie, no. Those are private files – "

"How long? How long have you known?" she snarled. She started taking framed photographs and awards down from the wall and crushing them under the heel of her boots.

"Good Lord, Ellie, let's just talk. Where is your mother? Does she know you're this upset?"

"Ha!" Ellie yelped. It was a sick, terrifying laugh, that emerged from the darkest recesses of her soul. "Does my mother *know?*" she mocked.

Jack looked as though he was going to use his walkie-talkie to call in some backup. Ellie lunged at him and ripped the unit from his hands.

"My mother, you sick, awful traitor, is *dead.*" She was seething so much that spittle was coming down her chin. "She's dead because of *you.*"

Her fists began to beat at his chest. His eyes widened at her words and then narrowed, the pummeling of her tired hands doing little to move or harm him. He grabbed both of her wrists and crossed them over and around to her back, causing her to yelp out in pain.

"Ellie. I won't hurt you. Just stop. Your mother…" he trailed off.

Suddenly exhausted, Ellie fell down to her knees and wrenched herself from his grasp. She rolled over onto her back and looked up at Jack. He stood still above her, running his hands over his face. He was white and gaunt, and his eyes stared into a reality that Ellie could not see.

"She's dead," Ellie repeated. "You killed her." Her voice began to crack. "I had to leave her." She heaved an angry breath. "I had to!" She began to softly weep. "I couldn't pull her out. I couldn't do it."

"But…but, they said…they said no one was there…they searched…the whole house, I made sure of it. I…I promise, Ellie, they…they were *sure!*" He continued running his hands back and forth over his cheeks, forehead, chin, lips.

"They were wrong," Ellie squeaked out. "Jack, they were wrong. She's dead."

Jack stumbled back and then fell to his knees. The sobs came quietly at first. His shoulders started to shake. Ellie sat up to take this in, the man who had killed her mother, weeping over her loss.

"What do you want, Jack?" Ellie asked, suddenly in full control of her emotions. "What are you after? What does my father have that you want so badly that you would kill my mother for it?"

"It's not what I want, Ellie, not what I want. It's never been what I want."

"You have to understand that I can trust no one."

Jack looked up at her, mournfully.

"I never wanted to do this, Ellie. They have me…they have me pinned. I had to protect you. I had to protect…I tried to protect…" his eyes filled with tears as he thought of Evelyn. He slumped against his desk, staring numbly out into space.

Ellie stood up from the ground. The entire space was littered with glass, papers, and random objects from her angry outburst. Below her foot she saw a photograph that looked like the photographs they had taken of Charlie behind the mill, but different in subject. She bent down to retrieve it and stood to study it in the light from the window.

She saw the side of the ARC truck and the two passengers who had jumped out. The security camera had full view of their faces, but the grainy quality of the photo left much to be desired. She didn't recognize either of them, nor did the image of the back of the mill worker's head give her any idea who these people were.

Her eyes settled on the driver, whose face was partially obstructed by the doorframe of the truck. She traced that familiar jawline, the set of those cheekbones, and the blazing fire rekindled itself instantly inside of her. She knew the man she was looking at. She knew him very well.

She was looking at her father.

Jack, still lost in his grief, did not see her slip the photograph inside her jacket to nestle beside the burlap bag.

She had to get to Mara, and she had to get to her now.

"Jack, what's next?" she asked, calmly. Jack looked up at her with so much guilt and sorrow, she could barely stand to look at him. "What happens to me now, Jack?"

He could barely get the words out. "I don't know, Ellie." His voice cracked. "I am still here for you." He paused. "I am your godfather."

"Meaning what? Now I have to live with you?"

Jack wiped the tears from his eyes and shrugged, forlorn.

Ellie thought of being in the same home with the man who had torn apart her family, the man who had caused her mother to gasp her last breaths - and she knew it would only be a matter of time before her grief would lead her to the knife block, or the gun cabinet, or the rat poison – and for whom, she scarcely knew. For herself? For him? For them both?

Though the idea of revenge felt sweet, sweeter than anything she had ever considered in her life, she clung to the knowledge that her father was alive, and that she wanted to see him again – and not from behind bars. She wanted to look him in the face, touch him, and then punch him for being so close to them and not coming home. He could have saved them. He could have prevented this. He could have changed this all.

"No, Jack. I can't do that. Not with you. Not now."

"Ells, we have time. Time to figure things out."

"What should I tell Mara? The truth? What even *is* the truth?"

He remained silent.

"You betrayed us, Jack. Not just me, not just Mara. All of us."

Ellie suddenly knew what she needed to do. She needed to go where they could all be back together. There was a way. She could see it now. She bent down to pick up the picture of Jack and her parents that he had kept on his desk for as long as she could remember. It had a hefty crack down the center of the glass but was otherwise intact. She placed it squarely on the lacquered wood in front of his leather chair.

"You won't be seeing me, Jack. But, if you ever get lonely," – she pointed at the photograph – "you've got your two best friends here to talk to."

She walked out of his office, her shoulders resolute, exiting into the bright but cold sunlight. The tulips in the window boxes that Gertie tended to were still green, but the edges of the slender heads were starting to turn pink. The daffodils swayed their happy little faces in the late March breeze.

She remembered the note from Charlie in her pocket as she strode along. Her fingers clamped around the key and squeezed it, remembering the way her heart had sunk hearing Jack speak his name. *He never meant anything. Everything he said was a lie.* She grabbed the note and key tightly in her fist, and, without opening the note, bent to drop them both down into the runoff grate on the side of the road. She heard them *plink* into the standing water below. *I will never trust him again.*

Her cheeks burned as she ran down the street.

Don't worry, Ellie-Belly. I've got you. Jack's strong arms had slithered underneath her and carried her from the floor of the barn back home. Her soaked clothing had dripped as they made their way across the field. Mother had walked alongside them, fretting and worried.

I don't know how she got herself down there, her mother said. *I mean, how did she lift that door?*

Ellie remembered the horrible haze that had clung to her for days. How she could not seem to get warm. How she had run over the events over and over and over again in her mind, positive that her mother had sent her to hide.

Ellie, she had said. *What on earth were you thinking?* Mother's hands were shaking. She looked away. Jack was around the house a lot that day. Her parents had talked in forceful whispers that night. Her mother had crept into her room after she thought Ellie was asleep and knelt by her bedside. *I'm so sorry,* she said. *I was trying to protect you. Someday you'll understand.*

Ellie arrived at her final destination. She opened the heavy glass doors, entered the brightly designed building, and headed straight for the reception desk. Her breath hung heavy in the air as she leaned across the counter. The handsome young man behind it leaned forward, a little taken back by her hurried entrance. "How can I help you?"

In that moment, all she had gone through, all that she knew, all that she wished, all that she wanted to take back – felt lighter than air, because she *knew*. She knew this was the last call, the only way, and that she was heading into the belly of the beast.

And when she got there, she was going to destroy it.

"Hi, José," Ellie said, grabbing a pen and squeezing it as she smiled. "I'm here to sign up."

ABOUT THE AUTHOR

D.H. Richards is a husband-and-wife writing team based in the Willamette Valley near Portland, OR. They run a happy and busy blended home of eight children and zero pets. It is their hope to raise people who think big and love even bigger. This is their first novel.

Made in the USA
Monee, IL
31 October 2020